MUTANT
MAMMOTHS
OF
MONTANA

Here's what readers from around the country are saying about Johnathan Rand's *AMERICAN CHILLERS:*

"I just read Terrible Tractors of Texas, and it was great! I live in Texas, and that book totally freaked me out!"

-Sean P., age 9, Texas

"I love your books! Can you make more so I can read them?"

-Alexis B., age 8, Michigan

"Last week, two kids in the library got into a fight over one of your books. But I don't remember what book it was."

-Kylee R., age 9, Nebraska

"I read The Haunted Schoolhouse in three days, and I'm reading it again! What a great book."

-Craig F., age 12, Florida

"I got Invisible Iguanas of Illinois for my birthday, and it's awesome! Write another one about Illinois!"

-Nick L., age 11, Illinois

"My brother says you're afraid of the dark, which is silly. But my brother makes things up a lot. I love your books, though!"

-Hope S., age 9, California

"I love your books! Make a book and put my name in it. That would be sweet!"

-Mark P., age 10, Montana

"I'm writing to tell you that THE MICHIGAN MEGA-MONSTERS was the scariest book I've ever read!"

-Clare H., age 11, Michigan

"In class, we read FLORIDA FOG PHANTOMS. I had never read your books before, but now I'm going to read all of them!"

-Clark D., age 8, North Carolina

"Our school library has all of your books, but they're always checked out. I have to wait two weeks to get OGRES OF OHIO. Can't you do something about that?"

-Abigail W., age 12, Minnesota

"When we visited Chillermania!, me and my brother met you! Do you remember? I had a red shirt on. Anyway, I bought DINOSAURS DESTROY DETROIT. It was great!"

-Carrie R., age 12, Ohio

"For school, we have to write to our favorite author. So I'm writing to you. If I get a letter back, my teacher says I can read it to the class. Can you send me a letter back? Not a long one, though. P.S. Everyone in my school loves your books!"

-Jim A., age 9, Arizona

"I LOVE AMERICAN CHILLERS!"

-Cassidy H., age 8, Missouri

"My mom is freaked out by the cover of POISONOUS PYTHONS PARALYZE PENNSYLVANIA. I told her if she really wanted to get freaked out, read the book! It's so scary I had to sleep with the light on!"

-Ally K., age 12, Tennessee

"Your books give me the chills! I really, really love them, but I don't know what one I like best."

-Jeff M., age 12, Utah

"I was read WISCONSIN WEREWOLVES, and now I'm freaked out, because I live in Wisconsin. I never knew we had werewolves."

-Angie T., age 9, Wisconsin

"I have every single AMERICAN CHILLER except VIRTUAL VAMPIRES OF VERMONT. I love all of them!"

-Cole H ., age 11, Michigan

"The lady at the bookstore told me I should read NEBRASKA NIGHTCRAWLERS, so I did. I just finished it, and it was GREAT!"

-Stephen S., age 8, Oklahoma

"SOUTH CAROLINA SEA CREATURES is the best book in the whole world!"

-Ashlee L, age 11, Georgia

"I read your books every night!"

-Aaron. W, age 10, New York

"I love your books! When I read AMERICAN CHILLERS, it's like I'm part of the story!"

-Leroy N., age 8, Rhode Island

"KREEPY KLOWNS OF KALAMAZOO is my favorite. It was awesome! I did a book report about it, and I got an 'A'!"

-Samantha T., age 10, Illinois

Don't miss these exciting, action-packed books by Johnathan Rand:

Michigan Chillers:
#1: Mayhem on Mackinac Island
#2: Terror Stalks Traverse City
#3: Poltergeists of Petoskey
#4: Aliens Attack Alpena
#5: Gargoyles of Gaylord
#6: Strange Spirits of St. Ignace
#7: Kreepy Klowns of Kalamazoo
#8: Dinosaurs Destroy Detroit
#9: Sinister Spiders of Saginaw
#10: Mackinaw City Mummies
#11: Great Lakes Ghost Ship
#12: AuSable Alligators
#13: Gruesome Ghouls of Grand Rapids
#14: Bionic Bats of Bay City

American Chillers:
#1: The Michigan Mega-Monsters
#2: Ogres of Ohio
#3: Florida Fog Phantoms
#4: New York Ninjas
#5: Terrible Tractors of Texas
#6: Invisible Iguanas of Illinois
#7: Wisconsin Werewolves
#8: Minnesota Mall Mannequins
#9: Iron Insects Invade Indiana
#10: Missouri Madhouse
#11: Poisonous Pythons Paralyze Pennsylvania
#12: Dangerous Dolls of Delaware
#13: Virtual Vampires of Vermont
#14: Creepy Condors of California
#15: Nebraska Nightcrawlers
#16: Alien Androids Assault Arizona
#17: South Carolina Sea Creatures
#18: Washington Wax Museum
#19: North Dakota Night Dragons
#20: Mutant Mammoths of Montana

Adventure Club series:
#1: Ghost in the Graveyard
#2: Ghost in the Grand
#3: The Haunted Schoolhouse

Freddie Fernortner, Fearless First Grader:

#1: The Fantastic Flying Bicycle
#2: The Super-Scary Night Thingy
#3: A Haunting We Will Go
#4: Freddie's Dog Walking Service
#5: The Big Box Fort
#6: Mr. Chewy's Big Adventure
#7: The Magical Wading Pool

#20: Mutant Mammoths of Montana

Johnathan Rand

An AudioCraft Publishing, Inc. book

This book is a work of fiction. Names, places, characters and incidents are used fictitiously, or are products of the author's very active imagination.

Book storage and warehouses provided by Chillermania!©
Indian River, Michigan

Warehouse security provided by:
Lily Munster and Scooby-Boo

American Chillers #20: Mutant Mammoths of Montana
ISBN 13-digit: 978-1-893699-79-3

Librarians/Media Specialists:
PCIP/MARC records available at www.americanchillers.com

Cover illustration by Dwayne Harris
Cover layout and design by Sue Harring

Printed in USA

MUTANT
MAMMOTHS
OF
MONTANA

VISIT CHILLERMANIA!

WORLD HEADQUARTERS FOR BOOKS BY JOHNATHAN RAND!

Yooperland

Indian River

Alpena

Traverse City

MICHIGAN

CHILLERMANIA!

*I-75 Exit 313
then south
1 mile!*

Mt. Pleasant

Bay City

Grand Rapids

Lansing

Detroit

Kalamazoo

Visit the HOME for books by Johnathan Rand! Featuring books, hats, shirts, bookmarks and other cool stuff not available anywhere else in the world! Plus, watch the American Chillers website for news of special events and signings at *CHILLERMANIA!* with author Johnathan Rand! Located in northern lower Michigan, on I-75! Take exit 313 . . . then south 1 mile! For more info, call (231) 238-0338. And be afraid! Be veeeery afraaaaaaiiiid . . . .

The alarm clock rang, jolting me awake. I slapped at it in the darkness until it stopped, then I fell back onto my pillow.

It was five a.m.

Although my bedroom door was closed, there was a thin band of light coming from beneath it. Mom and Dad were already up and moving about, getting ready for the day, packing our gear.

And I'm exhausted, I thought. *I can't believe I'm getting up this early.*

Oh, don't get me wrong. It was the first day of our camping vacation, and I had been excited for months. Every summer, we go somewhere fun. Last year, we went to Disneyland. The year before that, we went to California, where my cousins live. That's where my brother, Reese, fell and broke his arm.

But this year, we were staying in our home state of Montana. I remember the day Mom and Dad asked me about their idea. They'd been talking in the kitchen, then they came to my room and stood at the door. I was on my bed, reading a book, and I put it down and looked at them.

"Beth, what do you think about going on a camping trip this summer?" Mom asked.

"That would be cool!" I exclaimed. "Like . . . in a tent?"

Dad nodded. "Yes," he said. "We'll take two tents, and we'll use them for the whole week."

"And cook food over a fire?" I asked.

Mom and Dad nodded, smiling.

"That would be so much fun!" I exclaimed. "Have you asked Reese?"

"Not yet," Dad said. "But you know *him*. He loves the outdoors. I'm sure he'll be thrilled."

"Where are we going to go?" I asked.

"We haven't decided yet," Mom replied. "We wanted to make sure that you and your brother would want to do it."

"Are you kidding?!?!" I exclaimed as I sat up

and placed my feet on the floor. "Camping would be great!"

"Usually, we stay in hotels," Dad said, "but we thought it might be fun to explore the wilderness for a change. You know . . . do something different. Go for some hikes and do some exploring. I think it'll be fun, and we'll learn a lot about nature."

From that day forward, all I could think about was our upcoming camping trip. We looked through catalogs and went to sporting good stores to buy equipment. I got a new pair of hiking boots and a new windbreaker, along with a rain parka.

Then, one day, Mom and Dad decided where we were going to go: Glacier National Park.

Glacier National Park! I couldn't believe it! Glacier National Park is world famous! We live in Great Falls, Montana, which is about one hundred thirty miles away from the park . . . but we've never been there. Glacier National Park is huge: it has more than seven hundred miles of trails and is home to mountain goats, cougars, grizzly bears, and lots of other animals.

It also has twenty-seven glaciers, but they're melting fast. Dad says he read in the news that in thirty or forty years, all the glaciers in the park will probably have melted away.

I was really excited to camp at Glacier, but I was a little nervous . . . and maybe even a little scared.

Cougars? I thought. *Grizzly bears?*

While I thought it might be cool to see them, I wouldn't want to see them up close!

I needn't have worried. Cougars and grizzly bears were going to be the *least* of our troubles. Our troubles were going to be much bigger than that.

Several *tons* bigger, as a matter of fact.

2

After a few minutes of lying in bed and listening to the sounds of my mom and dad scurrying around the house, I sat up. My bedroom door opened, and light flooded in. The dark silhouette of my mom appeared.

"Rise and shine," she said as I raised my arm to cover my eyes from the harsh light that swamped my room.

I smiled thinly. "I'm awake," I replied.

"We'll be leaving at six," Mom said. "Double-check your gear, and make sure you have everything you need." She walked away, and I could hear shuffling around the house as she and Dad continued getting ready for our trip.

Too cool, I thought as I scrambled out of bed. I didn't think this day was ever going to get here.

After wolfing down a quick bowl of cereal, I went back to my room. I had made a list of all the things to take, but most of the stuff was already packed. I only needed to get things like toothpaste and soap.

Our plan was this: we would drive from our home in Great Falls to Glacier National Park. Dad said the trip would take us a couple of hours. From there, we would drive deep into the park to a place called Kintla Lake Campground. Kintla Lake Campground is located way up in the northwest corner in an area known as North Fork. Dad showed me the brochure. The campground was small; there were only about a dozen campsites, and the camping area was on the shores of Kintla Lake. Dad said that because it is so remote, there probably won't be too many other campers. But not far away was a small community called Polebridge, so if we needed supplies, we could go there.

At Kintla Lake Campground, we would set up our tents, and it would be our 'home base' for the entire week. From there, we would hike, fish, and explore. With so many miles of hiking trails, there would be plenty of things to do and plenty of things to see. Maybe even a grizzly bear.

So, you can imagine how excited I was. I was ready for seven whole days of adventure.

Our seven-day adventure, however, wasn't going to be anything like we thought. Sure, it would be filled with a lot of adventure.

But it would also be filled with something else: Terror.

3

The trip from Great Falls to Glacier was boring. We drove our van, which has a lot of room inside. Even with all our camping gear, I could still recline in my seat and stretch out. I fell asleep for a little while, but I woke up when Reese started poking me in the ribs. We got into an argument, but he was the one who started it. He always starts arguments. I never do. Anyway, he got into trouble for calling me a boogerhead, and Mom made him leave me alone. Then, I fell asleep again.

I was awakened by bright sunlight coming through the van window. I sat up and used my arm to shade my face. Outside, the van moved along a paved road. Trees and mountains rose into a perfect, blue sky. There were no other cars around.

Reese had fallen asleep in his seat. At some point, he'd eaten a chocolate bar, and he had a dab of brown goo around the edges of his mouth. He looked silly.

Mom was in the front passenger seat, and she turned. "Have a nice nap?" she asked.

"Yeah," I said with a yawn. "Where are we?"

"We're in the park already," Mom explained.

Holy cow, I thought. *I've slept nearly the entire trip!*

"So, how far are we from Kintla Lake Campground?" I asked.

"We still have a little ways to go," Dad replied. "We'll have to travel some bumpy roads to get there, so get ready."

While Reese slept, I turned and looked out the window. Everything was so scenic and beautiful, and I thought about all the things we would do over the next seven days. I had a new digital camera that was a birthday gift from Mom and Dad, so I planned to take a lot of pictures.

Soon, we were on a rugged, dirt road. The van bounced all around, waking Reese. When he first woke up, he looked silly. He was groggy, and he still had chocolate goo around his mouth. He didn't know it, though, and I wasn't going to tell him.

"Where . . . where are we?" he stammered as he balled his fists and rubbed his eyes.

"We're almost home," I teased. "They don't allow goofy boys at the park, so we had to take you back."

Reese didn't say anything. Instead, he stuck his tongue out at me.

Typical Reese, I thought, turning to look out my window.

At that very moment, I saw something at the edge of the forest. At first, I couldn't believe it.

I *wouldn't* believe it.

I was looking at a *monster!*

At first, I thought I was looking at a rock formation. As we bounced along the road, the trees were set back a little, and there were some big rocks and boulders nestled along the edge of the forest. Behind and above the trees, larger, jagged mountains loomed.

But a certain large boulder (at least, that's what I *thought* it was, at first) looked out of place.

Like it didn't belong.

And then I could make out a mouth.

And eyes.

I could see two long tusks, like a bull elephant, and enormous ears. The thing was covered with thick, reddish-brown fur that was matted and dirty.

And its legs were gigantic, the size of tree trunks! They, too, looked liked elephant legs, except they appeared to have claws like that of a bear. But it was no elephant, that was for sure. And besides: what would an elephant be doing in Montana?

Suddenly, we went around a bend in the road, and I could no longer see the creature.

"Did . . . did anyone else see that?!?!" I blurted.

"See what?" Mom asked.

"Dad, stop!" I said. "I saw something back there!"

"What?" Dad asked.

"I don't know!" I said. "But it looked like an elephant . . . except it was bigger and uglier!"

This brought a round of laughter from everyone: Mom, Dad, and Reese.

"No, really!" I pleaded. "There was some big animal back there! I *saw* it with my own eyes!"

"There aren't any animals in the park that big," Mom said. "Maybe it was a moose."

"I know a moose when I see one," I said, and it was true. We have moose in Montana, and I see them once in a while.

I turned all the way around in my seat, straining against the seatbelt. I was hoping to get another glimpse of whatever it was . . . but we were too far away, and there were too many trees.

Maybe it was just my imagination, I thought. *Maybe it was nothing. After all . . . I just woke up. Maybe I'm still sleepy.*

And that's what I told myself. I told myself that I had imagined the strange creature at the edge of the forest. I told myself that Mom was right: there aren't any animals that big in Glacier National Park. In fact, there aren't animals that big *anywhere* in America . . . except in zoos and circuses.

I wouldn't be telling myself that for long. Soon, we'd know the truth . . . and our camping trip to Glacier National Park was going to turn into a fight for our lives!

5

When we reached Kintla Lake Campground, I'd forgotten all about the thing I'd spotted in the trees. I'd convinced myself it was just my imagination, and I didn't think any more of it.

As I tumbled out of the van, I couldn't believe how beautiful everything was. The lake was clear and blue, and mountain peaks jutted into a sky that was just as blue as the lake. Green trees grew thick, and the air was clean and smelled of sticky pine.

And Dad was right: the campground was remote. In fact, there were no other campers around anywhere.

"Where is everybody?" Reese asked as he climbed from the van.

"Oh, more campers will come along, I'm sure," Dad replied. "But this is one of the smaller campgrounds, so there probably won't be too many people around. Besides . . . we're a long way from anywhere, except Polebridge. Come on, guys . . . let's unload our gear and set up camp."

It took a few hours of hard work to get our camp set up. We had two tents: Mom and Dad had a bigger one you could stand up in, while Reese and I had a smaller, two-person tent that gave us just enough room for our two sleeping bags. While we set it up, Reese and I talked about wild animals.

"I hope we see a cougar!" he exclaimed.

I shook my head. "I doubt it," I said. "They're too clever, and they stay away from people if they can."

"I think it would be cool to have one as a pet," he said.

"You're crazy!" I said. But I had to admit: it would be great to see a cougar . . . from a long way away, of course.

"And there are bears around, too," Reese said.

"Grizzly bears and black bears."

That was another thing we had to remember. There was a chance we might come across a bear, and we had to know what to do. Dad had told us how to act and what to do. Two of the most important things, he said, was to stick together when we were hiking and make noise. Bears don't like humans, and they'll stay away if they can. By making noise, it alerts the bears that there are people around, and they can stay away.

There were other things we had to do, too. Bears have really good noses and can smell food from great distances. Dad said we'd keep our food in the van so the bears wouldn't be able to get it, and that we couldn't leave any scraps lying around the campsite . . . or anywhere else, for that matter. He told us to be sure to pick up after ourselves, and that it was important to leave our campsite even cleaner than we'd found it, so other people could enjoy it.

There were other rules, of course, but we'd been talking about our trip for weeks, and I was sure I was prepared.

In fact, I *knew* I was prepared.

For everything.

But nothing could have prepared me for what I would discover only a few hundred feet from our campsite . . . .

After we got our campsite in order, Reese and I walked down to the lake. It was the most beautiful sight I think I've ever seen! The water was clean and clear, and so was the sky. The air smelled fresh and crisp.

And I was so excited! We've camped outside in our backyard at home, but this would be the first time we ever went camping for *real*. Oh, camping in our backyard was fun. We often made a fire and roasted marshmallows, and Dad would tell ghost stories. Some of his stories were pretty cheesy, but some of them were pretty good. Even Mom had some good ghost stories.

But this was totally different. Here, we were away from the city. At night, we wouldn't look up to see street lights and power lines, but, rather, the silhouettes of trees and mountains in the distance. There would be billions of twinkling stars to see. We might even hear the howling of a wolf!

Reese and I stood at the edge of the lake, just staring. With no one else around, it was like having the mountains and the trees and the sky all to ourselves.

"This is so cool," he whispered.

We walked back to our campsite, where Dad was still busy arranging things in their tent. Mom was getting dinner ready, which was going to be simple: hot dogs and macaroni and cheese. My favorite! I could eat macaroni and cheese until it came out of my ears.

While we were still settling into camp, I heard a vehicle approach. I turned to see a brown park ranger truck. It stopped in front of our campsite, and a ranger wearing a brown uniform got out.

"Howdy, folks," he said. "You all right?"

Which I thought was strange. Why would he ask a question like that?

Dad approached the ranger, and they shook hands. "Yeah, we're fine," Dad said. "What's wrong?"

"Well, we had a little earthquake this morning," the ranger replied.

"An earthquake?!?!" Reese shouted. *"Really?"*

The park ranger nodded. "Never had one in these parts before, as far as I can tell. Scared a lot of campers away, but no one was hurt. I don't think there's anything to worry about."

"We just got here a little while ago," Mom said. "We don't know a thing about it."

"It was early this morning," the ranger said. "You were probably too far away to feel it. Still, I just want to check on everyone in this area and make sure they're all right. Lots of people got scared and left, though. But, like I said: I don't think there's anything to worry about."

The ranger said good-bye and left.

"An earthquake," Reese said, shaking his head. "Man . . . I miss all the good stuff."

When we finished dinner, I walked down to the lake. After a few minutes, Reese showed up with his fishing pole. He fished for a couple of hours, but he didn't catch anything.

When it got dark, we sat around the campfire. The night air was cool, so we wore our sweatshirts. Dad told us a ghost story about a haunted train. He said the story was true, but I learned long ago not to believe him when he was telling one of his ghost stories.

Then, we went to bed, where I fell asleep quickly. It had been a long day, and as soon as I crawled into my sleeping bag, I was snoozing.

But I was awakened sometime later by my brother. He had me by the shoulder, and he was shaking me.

"Beth!" he hissed. *"Beth! Wake up! Did you hear that?!?!"*

Now, my brother is a year younger than I am, but he doesn't get scared often. However, I could tell by his voice that, this time, he was *horrified.*

7

"What?" I replied groggily. "What time is it?"

"I don't know," Reese replied. "But it's still dark. You didn't hear that sound?"

"I was sleeping," I said. "I didn't hear a thing."

"It was really weird," Reese said. "Listen."

We listened for a moment, but the only thing we heard was the rhythmic chirping of crickets. Nothing else.

"What was it?" I asked.

"I don't know," Reese replied. "It sounded like an elephant, but not really."

"What's that *supposed* to mean?" I whispered.

35

"Well, it was sort of a trumpeting sound, but sort of a growl, too. It sounded far away, but it was freaky."

"Well, if it was far away," I said, *"there's nothing to worry about. Go back to sleep."*

And that's what we did. In fact, in the morning, I forgot all about Reese waking me up and telling me about the sound. He'd forgotten about it, too . . . until we were all seated around the fire, eating breakfast. Dad made eggs, bacon, and toast, and it was delicious.

"Hey!" Reese suddenly said. "Did anyone hear that noise last night?"

Mom and Dad looked at him and shook their heads. "What noise?" Dad asked.

"I don't know what it was," Reese said as he popped a small piece of bacon into his mouth. "But it sounded weird. Like a growling elephant, a long ways away."

"There aren't any elephants in Glacier National Park," Dad said.

"I know," Reese replied. "But it sounded like one. A growling elephant."

"Are you sure you weren't dreaming?" Mom asked.

"Oh, I was awake, all right," Reese said. "I even

woke up Beth, but she didn't hear the noise."

And that was that. Reese didn't talk again about the noise he'd heard the night before, and the matter was dropped. We talked about other things: hiking, animals, fishing . . . things like that. Dad said that we'd spend the day settling in and set out for a hike the next day. There were lots of trails all over the place, and I was looking forward to exploring some of the park.

Meanwhile, Reese and I decided to do a little exploring on our own . . . and that's how this whole mess got started. I was excited, as I was hoping to see some cool wild animals and birds. I had no idea we were about to encounter the strangest beasts the world has ever known.

Reese and I washed and put away the breakfast pans and dishes. Then, we prepared our backpacks. Oh, we didn't plan to be gone long. We weren't even going to go very far, but it would still be fun to carry our packs. I filled mine with some of the things I'd brought: a flashlight, my first aid kit, a book of matches, a rain poncho, a pencil, an apple, a bottle of water, and my digital camera. Reese had the same items, except he didn't have a camera. Also, he packed his video game.

"Why in the world would you take a video game on a hike?" I asked him.

He shrugged. "I don't know," he said. "In case I get bored. Then, I've got something to do."

I shook my head. It seemed silly to take something like that on a camping trip. Oh, I have a video game, too . . . but I left it at home. I figured I'd be too busy with other things. Besides: I can play video games any day of the week, if I want.

Dad gave us a small map of the campground, and told us not to go far.

"Remember," he said, "this is a big park. If you don't stay on the trails, it'll be easy to get lost. So, don't wander off. And the weather report is calling for a thunderstorm. Storms here can come up fast, so if you see dark clouds, head back to camp."

"Okay," I said. "We won't go far."

Mom was sitting in a lawn chair, reading a book in the shade. "And be back at noon for lunch," she said. "Do you have your watch on?"

"I do," I said.

"I left mine at home," Reese replied.

Off we went. The morning sun was warming the air, and everything smelled fresh and new. Reese and I hiked down to the lake. Again, I gazed at the surroundings, marveling at how beautiful everything was. In the lake I saw a fish jump, and I wondered if we'd catch any of them during the course of the week.

"Let's head that way," Reese said, pointing to a trail that wound alongside the lake.

"Go for it," I said, and we set out. I followed Reese, and we walked along the rocky trail. I kept my eyes out for animals and birds. I saw a rabbit, but nothing else.

After hiking a few hundred yards, Reese stopped. The trail continued to wind around the lake, but another trail headed into the forest, up a steep hill. Beyond that, I could see several small rock formations climbing up into the sky.

"Let's go that way, up that hill," Reese said.

"Fine with me," I replied. "Let's just stay on the trail so we don't get lost."

We hiked up the hill. At the top, the terrain flattened a little, but soon, we were again hiking up yet another steep hill, around large rocks and boulders. When I turned to look behind me, I saw Kintla Lake all blue and beautiful and the majestic mountains beyond.

"I sure would like to know what made that sound last night," Reese said as he walked. "I've never heard anything like it before."

"Maybe it was a cougar," I said.

That made Reese nervous, and he stopped hiking. He looked around. "Yeah," he said. "I forgot that there are cougars in the park. I really hope we don't see one of those."

"Wait a minute," I said. "Back at camp, you said you hoped to see a cougar."

"Well, I mean, I hope to see one . . . if he's far away. I wouldn't want to see one up close."

We hiked on, weaving around huge rocks and trees, up and down hills, making sure we stayed on the trail.

And by this time, I'd forgotten all about the strange thing I'd spotted in the woods the day before. In fact, I was convinced it was nothing more than trees and rocks and my imagination. Not once did I think the sound Reese had heard could have been connected with the thing I *thought* I saw.

However, we were about to find something that would make us realize there were creatures in the forest that weren't supposed to be there. And it all started when I looked into the woods and spotted something on a tree branch only a few yards from the trail . . . .

"Look at that!" I said excitedly. I pointed.

"What is it?" Reese asked.

"See? On that branch over there! It's a butterfly!"

"Big deal," Reese said, rolling his eyes. "I thought it was something cool."

"It's a tiger swallowtail," I said. "It would be cool to get a picture of him."

I slipped the pack off my back and dug out my digital camera. Then, I put my pack back on, figuring I might just as well carry my camera in my hand where it would be handy. That way, if I saw something else

I wanted to shoot with my camera, I wouldn't have to waste any more time. I didn't want to miss taking a picture of something because I'd spent too much time getting my camera.

I raised the camera and stepped off the trail. The butterfly didn't move.

"Hey, remember what Dad told us about leaving the trail," Reese warned. "This is a National Park. We aren't supposed to leave the trail."

"I'm not going very far," I said. "I just want to get a picture of the butterfly."

I walked slowly. Twigs crunched beneath my feet, and tall grass licked at my bare legs. Both Reese and I were wearing shorts because the day was supposed to be hot, just like the day before.

The butterfly remained on the branch. I took another step toward him, then another. I could see him in my camera's viewfinder, but I wanted to get as close as I could.

I must have spooked him, because the butterfly suddenly flitted into the air. I thought he was gone for good, but he landed on a branch not far away.

No problem, I thought. *I'll just move a little slower.*

I walked toward the insect. A few tree branches were in my way, and I pushed them aside with my free hand while holding my digital camera in front of me.

"Beth," Reese called out from behind me.

"Don't worry," I said. "I'm not going far." I turned to look behind me and was surprised to find I couldn't see my brother. Oh, I wasn't very far away from him or the trail, but I'd traveled far enough that tree branches and saplings prevented me from seeing him.

I turned my attention to the tiger swallowtail. His yellow and black wings glowed in the morning sunshine. I think tiger swallowtails are the prettiest butterflies I have ever seen.

I took a picture, but it didn't come out very well. I was still too far away.

I crept closer. I moved slowly, not wanting to spook the butterfly again. This time, I was able to get within a couple of feet from him. The entire butterfly filled my camera's viewfinder, and I took a picture. As soon as I did, the insect fluttered from the branch, rose into the air, and vanished.

I pressed the playback mode on my camera. The picture was *perfect!* It was crisp and clear and showed the whole butterfly! I couldn't wait to take it to school in the fall so I could show my new teacher and all my friends. Of course, I would have a *lot* of pictures from my camping trip!

I shut the camera off and was about to return to the trail, when I looked down.

Something in the earth struck me as odd. At first, I didn't realize what I was seeing. When I did, however, a wave of fear rushed over me.

"Reese!" I screamed. *"Come here! Quick!"*

I heard branches snap and brush moving behind me, but I couldn't tear my eyes away from what I was seeing on the ground at my feet.

"Beth!" Reese shouted. *"What is it?!?! What's wrong?!?!"*

"Over here!" I replied, still staring at the ground. *"You've got to see this!"*

Reese emerged through the brush with twigs, leaves, and pine needles in his hair. He pulled them out.

"What's wrong?" he asked. "Why did you yell?"

"Look!" I said, pointing to the ground.

At first, he didn't know what he was looking at. Then, he took a step backward and his jaw dropped so fast that I thought it was going to break! I knew he was seeing the same thing I was:

A giant track of some animal, nearly four feet long! It was very strange looking and pressed into the earth several inches. Obviously, it was some sort of footprint . . . but whatever it was, it had very long claws that dug into the dirt. I knew of no animal on earth that could make a footprint that big. Not even an elephant!

"That's impossible!" Reese said. "That must be fake. Someone must've created that thing on their own to fool people."

"But why here?" I asked. "Why did they do it back in the woods? Why not closer to the trail, where more people would see it? And look!" I pointed a few feet ahead of the footprint. "There's another one!"

Sure enough, there was another footprint in the ground. And ahead of it was another!

Reese looked around, and he picked up on something I hadn't noticed. "Look at these tree branches," he said. "They're all snapped off, like something big broke them."

"What in the world could *possibly* make tracks that big?" I said. "There's no animal in the world big enough!"

We knelt down and studied the tracks. I could make out what appeared to be a giant foot at the base of the claw marks. It was a foot of some sort, all right . . . but what did the track belong to?

Maybe Reese is right, I thought. *Maybe someone did it as a joke, just to fool people. Still . . . if it's someone's idea of a prank, why did they do it way out here, in the forest, where most people wouldn't even see the tracks? Why not do it near the campground where there were more people around?*

It didn't make sense.

We got to our feet.

"Well, whatever made the tracks," Reese said, "it must be big." He pointed up and around. "Look at all the broken tree branches. Whatever came through here was big enough to snap trees in half."

Around us, there were many broken tree limbs, some of them ten feet off the ground. Some trees hadn't been broken, but were bent and twisted sideways, as if they had been pushed out of the way.

"Well, there's only one way to find out," I said.

"Let's follow the tracks."

Reese looked at me with wide eyes. "No way," he said, shaking his head. "You *know* what Dad told us. He said to stay on the trail."

Sure, Reese was right. Dad *had* warned us not to leave the trail. But I really wanted to find out what sort of creature could make tracks that big . . . if they were actually from a real creature, after all.

"Yeah, I know," I said. "But think about it: if we follow the footprints, we won't get lost. All we'll have to do is follow them back to where we are now. The trail is right over there. There's no way we can get lost."

I could tell my brother wasn't sure. But I'm his older sister, and he usually listens to me.

"I don't know," he said.

"Look," I said, trying my best to convince him. "Let's just follow these tracks for five minutes. If we don't find anything, we'll come back."

Finally, he relented. "All right," Reese said. But I knew he thought it wasn't a good idea.

Turns out, he would be right.

And so would Dad. You see, sometimes the rules my parents make for us seem silly, and I don't understand them—Mom and Dad, or the rules they make—until later. Then, I usually find out that the rules are because they don't want us to get hurt or get into trouble.

But not this time. I knew we wouldn't get into trouble, and I knew we wouldn't get lost. I knew nothing would happen.

Oh, if only I would have listened to what Dad had told us, we would never have gotten into the trouble we were about to.

The footprints were easy to follow. Even if we couldn't see any tracks (and in some places we couldn't, because the ground was solid rock), there was evidence of where the animal had passed by. Branches and limbs had been broken, and some small trees had been knocked over.

"Whatever made these tracks and snapped these trees," I said, "it sure is big."

"Maybe we shouldn't be following the tracks, after all," Reese said. "Maybe we should get Mom and Dad. Or tell a park ranger."

"Let's just go a little ways farther," I said. I

stopped walking, looked ahead, and pointed. "Let's hike to the top of that ridge," I said. "That's where the tracks are headed. If we get to the top of the ridge and don't see anything, we'll head back."

"Okay," Reese said reluctantly, and we started walking again.

Now, you have to understand I *was* a little freaked out, but I was so curious about what made the footprints that I just *had* to know what kind of animal made them.

Suddenly, I stopped.

"Wait a minute!" I said. "Yesterday, on our way here, I saw something in the woods. Something huge! Remember?"

"Yeah, but that was your imagination," Reese said. "Even you *yourself* said that."

I pointed to one of the giant footprints. "Does *this* look like my imagination?" I asked. "Something made these tracks, and whatever it is, it's got to be gigantic."

We kept walking and glancing around warily, wondering if we would get a glimpse of whatever had made the enormous footprints. Finally, we reached the ridge.

"Well, so much for that," Reese said, throwing up his hands. "Whatever made those tracks is probably long gone by now. Maybe on the other side of Montana."

From where we were, we could see far into the distance. I could see all of Kintla Lake and mountains reaching up into the blue sky, which had only a few white, puffy clouds. Green trees covered the countryside, among jagged, gray rock formations. Again, I marveled at how beautiful everything was.

"Let's head back," Reese said. "There's *got* to be better things to do."

And that's when I saw something that seemed odd. Something out of place, something that didn't fit.

I pointed. "Look over there," I said. "It looks like a cave at the bottom of that cliff."

Reese looked where I was pointing. He shrugged. "So?" he said. "I'm sure there are caves all over the place."

"But look at those rocks," I said. Around the entrance of the cave, there were big boulders. However, some of the boulders had fallen on trees and snapped them. The leaves on the trees were still green, so that meant the boulders had crushed the trees recently, since the trees weren't dead yet. I wondered if the earthquake had shaken the rocks loose, causing them to tumble down.

"You've seen one cave, you've seen them all," Reese said impatiently. "Are you ready to go, or what?"

"But look," I said, "look at the footprints. They lead right to that big cave."

"Even more reason to head back," Reese said.

I shook my head. "Let's go check it out," I said.

Reese shook his head. "I don't want to," he said.

"I think you're a chicken," I said. "I think you're afraid."

"I am not!" Reese said. "I just don't want to go."

"Tell you what," I said. "Let's just go take a peek inside the cave. You're probably right: there's probably nothing to see. If so, I *promise* we'll head back."

Reese thought about this for a moment. "Promise?" he said.

I drew an invisible 'X' over my chest with my right index finger. "Cross my heart," I said.

"Oh, all right," Reese said. "But just to the cave. No farther."

"Just to the cave," I agreed, and we started out.

We didn't have far to hike. However, as we got closer to the dark opening, I started to get nervous, and I didn't know why. I just felt a little jittery, like something was about to happen.

And, I must admit, I *was* a little scared. After all: the tracks we were following were obviously made by some giant animal. Maybe one that had never before been spotted by any human!

We approached the cave slowly, because we had to climb over and around several big boulders. Finally, we were standing at the entrance. The mouth of the cave was huge! From the ridge where we'd been standing earlier, it hadn't looked as big as it actually was.

We stared into the cave, looking around. There really wasn't much to see. Neither of us spoke for a full minute.

"See?" Reese finally said. "There's nothing in the cave. Let's go home."

Reese was right. There was nothing in the cave.

It was the thing coming up behind us, through the woods, that we would have to worry about.

12

At first, nothing seemed out of the ordinary. Looking into the cave, nothing particularly strange caught my attention, except the fact that rocks had snapped some trees nearby.

"I'll bet that earthquake caused the earth to open up and form this," I said, pointing to the large boulders around the mouth of the cave. "It doesn't look like it's been too long since those rocks crushed the trees."

"And those tracks go inside the cave," Reese said, pointing.

I took a few steps closer. Now, I was almost

inside the cave. "Not only that," I said, "but it looks like there are more tracks going out! Look at all of these footprints!"

They were everywhere. The earth around the mouth of the cave was a mixture of dark dirt and rocks, but it was easy to see that whatever the animal was, there was more than one of them.

"This is freaking me out," Reese said. "I think we should go back and tell Mom and Dad."

"In a minute," I said. I was still carrying my digital camera, and I raised it up. I found one of the strange footprints in the viewfinder and clicked a picture. Then, I took several more. That's what I like about my new digital camera: I can take hundreds of pictures and not have to worry about running out of film. I can download them to our computer at home and only print the ones I want.

"Wait until we show everyone what we found!" I said.

Just then, I heard a loud snap from behind us. Reese and I turned, but we didn't see anything.

"What was that?" he asked.

I shrugged. "I don't know," I said.

"You know," Reese said nervously, "I'm not sure

I want to see the animals that made these tracks. What if they're dangerous?"

We heard another noise, and I was sure it was a large tree branch snapping. Still, we couldn't see anything.

Reese was getting scared. "I don't like this," he said. "I think we should get out of here."

Another noise came from the forest. Not far away, in a valley, I saw a couple of trees move.

Now, it was my turn to get nervous. Reese made a good point: what if the animal was dangerous? Whatever created those footprints had to be enormous. What if it wasn't friendly?

"Let's hide," I said, after I saw a couple more trees in the distance shudder and shake. One tree looked like it was knocked down . . . but it was still too far away to see what caused it.

"Where?" Reese asked.

"Let's duck behind that rock over there," I said, and we rushed to one of the large boulders at the mouth of the cave. I peeked around the side of the rock, holding out my digital camera, ready to take a picture.

The snapping of trees and branches grew

louder. A tree snapped, and it sounded like a shotgun going off.

"Can you see anything yet?" Reese whispered. He was kneeling on the ground next to me, but he wasn't looking. He was really frightened.

"Not yet," I whispered back.

Suddenly, we heard a loud noise. It wasn't really a trumpeting, but a long, squealing growl. It sent a shiver up and down my spine.

"That's what I heard last night!" Reese hissed. *"That's the sound I heard!"*

All at once, several trees near a clearing bent over and snapped.

I was holding the camera up, ready to take a picture, but when I saw what was emerging from the forest, I was shaking so badly I couldn't even press the button. I suddenly felt very cold.

Reese must've seen my shocked expression. *"What?"* he asked. *"What do you see?"*

I couldn't talk. I couldn't even whisper. The only thing I could do . . . was scream.

13

What I was seeing was something from the pages of a science textbook—sort of. The creature that emerged from the forest was a mammoth, only it was very different from the paintings and drawings I'd seen in books. It was bigger than an elephant and had long, dark brown hair. Two long, cream-colored tusks curled out from his jaws, just like a mammoth. But his legs and feet were very strange. They weren't like the legs of an elephant at all, but, rather, like large pads with long claws. And it had a long trunk, but with tentacles instead of a snout. It was the strangest thing I think I'd ever seen in my life.

"Oh . . . my . . . gosh," I whispered. Each word came out slowly, and I didn't recognize my own voice.

"What is it?" Reese asked. He poked his head over my shoulder and sucked in a deep breath. *"Holy smokes!"* he shouted, and he nearly blew out my eardrum.

The mammoth—or whatever it was—also heard Reese's shout. He stopped and looked in our direction. His trunk rose into the sky, and the odd-looking tentacles swarmed in the air like live snakes.

And I knew we were looking at the same creature I had spotted on our way to our campsite yesterday, when I was in the van. This was the creature I'd seen! I just didn't get a good look at it yesterday, as we passed by in the vehicle. Now, seeing the creature out in the open, I had a clear view, and I knew I wasn't imagining things. After all: Reese was seeing the mammoth, too.

But now we had another problem: the creature heard us and was staring us down.

"Don't move," I whispered.

"I don't think I could if I tried," Reese replied.

We waited, motionless, against the large boulder. The mammoth-creature didn't move—except for his trunk, which was raised in the air and swaying back and forth. The tentacles at the end of his trunk were swirling and whirling slowly, and I wondered if that's how the creature picked up scents. Maybe the tentacles were used to pick up smells.

I don't know if he smelled us or not, but the mammoth began moving, slowly walking toward us. Suddenly, I realized the mistake we'd made. We'd hidden near the rock, which wasn't so bad . . . but now that the mammoth was coming our way, we had nowhere to go but inside the cave. I don't know if we could have outrun the mammoth if we needed to, but right now, we had no option but to go into the cave and hope to find another place to hide . . . if the mammoth kept walking toward us.

Well, I didn't have to worry about that, because suddenly, the mammoth stopped walking—and started running!

He had spotted us, and he was charging!

Without even thinking about it, Reese and I spun and ran into the cave. It grew dark quickly, but there were several large rocks that could provide cover. That is, of course, unless the mammoth came into the cave.

We ducked behind the boulders. We were inside the cave, but we were still able to see outside. The ground trembled and shook as the monstrous creature came closer.

"Get your flashlight out!" I said to Reese. "If we have to go farther into the cave, at least we'll be able to see!"

I tucked my digital camera into my pocket.

Then, I slipped my backpack off and dropped it on the ground at my feet, glad that I had brought not only my pack, but the items I had chosen. I never thought I'd be using my flashlight on our hike, but I'd brought it along simply because I had the extra space in my pack.

Reese slipped his backpack off and pulled out his flashlight. All the while, the ground trembled and shook under the weight of the charging mammoth.

"Get ready!" I said as I slipped my backpack on. "We might have to go farther into the cave!"

"But, what if that thing comes in after us?!?!" Reese asked. He, too, put his backpack on. "What do we do?"

I didn't have an answer. "I don't know," I said. "We can only hope that the mammoth will be too big to come into the cave."

While we watched, the giant creature thundered closer and closer. Then, he slowed to a steady gallop. Soon, he wasn't running, but walking. The earth shook with every step he took.

Soon, the giant beast was standing at the mouth of the cave. He was so big he blocked much of the daylight, and our surroundings grew dim.

But the bad news was that he wasn't so big he

couldn't come into the cave if he wanted, and that made me nervous. I didn't want to have to go deeper into the cave unless we really had to.

We watched the mammoth. Once again, he extended his trunk into the air. The strange tentacles on his snout swirled about, and I was now certain he was using them to try to sniff us out.

"What's he doing?" Reese whispered.

"I think he's trying to smell us," I replied quietly.

"That's the freakiest looking thing I've ever seen in my life!" Reese hissed.

Suddenly, the huge mammoth raised one of his front legs. He pawed at the ground with his long claws.

Then, he took a step forward. His trunk was still extended, swishing slowly back and forth between his enormous tusks.

Then, he took another step.

And another.

He was coming inside the cave!

15

"*Run!*" I hissed.

Reese and turned and fled. Quickly, it became too dark to see. I clicked on my flashlight just in time: I was about to run straight into a large rock, which would have tripped me up for sure. I leapt around it and kept going.

The cave turned to the right and angled down a little, but I noticed it was still very big. If the mammoth-creature wanted to come after us, he wouldn't have any trouble.

"What does that thing want?" Reese asked as we sprinted through the dark cavern. We had to be careful, because there were rocks everywhere. However, for the most part, we were running on hard-packed ground and loose gravel. Our shoes made crunching sounds as we ran, and our steps echoed off the walls of the cave. If the creature was after us, we wouldn't be able to hear him.

But I didn't feel the earth trembling, so I hoped that maybe he was going to leave us alone.

Fat chance of that.

We had just rounded another corner in the cave and I slowed, thinking we were far enough away. Reese slowed, too, but then we heard—and felt—the mammoth coming. We had no way of knowing how far away he was, but he was still after us, that was for sure.

We were about to start running again when Reese shouted.

"Wait!" he exclaimed. He shined his flashlight to the right. "There's a smaller tunnel, right there! It won't be big enough for that thing to go through!"

He was right! There was a dark passage that was much smaller than the tunnel we were in. There was no way the mammoth-creature would be able to get at us.

"Let's go!" I said. "Hurry!"

Reese ducked into the narrow cavern, and I was right behind him. The tunnel was small and was just barely wide enough for us to squeeze into. In fact, it was a tight fit, like we were squeezed into a thin, narrow closet. Plus, the top of the cave wasn't very high, and if I was any taller, I would have hit my head or had to crouch down.

All too late, we realized we'd made a terrible mistake. While the tunnel was too small for the mammoth to enter, it dead-ended after several feet! The tunnel went nowhere.

"Maybe there's another tunnel!" I cried. "Look for it!"

We swept our flashlight beams all around us, but there was nothing to see but jagged rock.

"At least that ugly thing can't get us," Reese said. "He's too big."

Reese was right, of course. The mammoth was far too big to come after us in such a small space.

Unfortunately, we forgot one important thing: the mammoth's trunk. It was long and narrow, and the mammoth could easily use it to get at us.

And that's exactly what the creature did!

16

We didn't even have time to catch our breath. We heard a loud crunching of gravel, and the ground beneath us shook. I knew the mammoth was coming, but I was hoping we'd outsmarted him and he would pass on by.

No such luck.

The creature stopped right at the entrance of our narrow hiding place. I quickly clicked off my flashlight.

"Turn your light off!" I whispered to Reese. *"Maybe he won't see us!"*

Reese turned off his flashlight, and everything

got very dark. In fact, I'd never been in such inky blackness. Even in my bedroom at night, with the door closed, there's still a little light. The digits of my clock glow green, and there's a night light in the hall that glows beneath my door. Even outside on dark nights, there are stars or the moon or streetlights.

But here, in a cave deep in the ground, there was nothing to see. However, we could *hear* . . . and that's what *really* frightened me. The mammoth wasn't moving around much, but I could hear loud sniffing sounds. I was sure he *must* know where we were hiding, and I'd forgotten about his trunk . . . until I felt something on my arm! It was wet and slimy, and I drew back, squishing Reese against the hard rock behind me with my backpack.

"Ouch!" he cried. "Watch it! You're crushing me!"

"That thing's nose is touching me!" I screeched, and I wiped my hand on my arm where the mammoth had touched me. "Eewww!" I shouted. "I've got mammoth boogers on my arm!"

The thing kept trying to touch me, and I clicked on my flashlight so I could see. I was so grossed-out by the mammoth boogers on my arm I forgot that what I was doing might be dangerous. I began using the flashlight to strike out at the beast's trunk, hoping it would leave me alone.

It worked! The mammoth's trunk gave off a deep snorting sound, then retreated like a departing snake.

"This is the grossest thing that's ever happened to me in my whole life!" I shouted, still wiping the mammoth boogers from my arm. "This is totally, totally *gross!*"

"Better you than me," Reese said.

At the entrance of our hiding place, the mammoth moved. I stopped rubbing my arm and trained the flashlight beam ahead of me.

A horrible, evil eye came into view. It was black and glossy, about the size of a softball.

He was looking at us.

Watching us.

Waiting.

After all, we couldn't go anywhere, and the mammoth probably knew it. His trunk wasn't quite long enough to grab one of us, and I didn't think he would be able to get at us with one of his tusks.

Soon, however, the creature began to move. I

could hear him moving away, farther along the tunnel.

Which meant—

We could get out!

If the creature kept going, we would be able to leave our tight quarters and run in the opposite direction. In less than sixty seconds, we could be back in the daylight again!

"Let's wait for a minute," I told Reese. "Let's wait until we can't hear him anymore, then we'll make our escape."

A few minutes passed, and I decided it was safe enough to make a run for it.

"Ready?" I asked Reese, who was still behind me, pressed against the rock.

"I was ready five minutes ago," Reese said.

"Turn your light on," I said. "And remember: once we start running, don't stop until you get outside."

"Are you kidding?!?!" Reese said. "I'm not stopping until we get to our campsite! I might not even stop until I get to Texas!"

"Come on," I said, and I shuffled to the entrance of the narrow tunnel that had been our hiding place. I shined my flashlight beam all around the larger, more spacious cavern. I saw nothing except sharp rock walls and stony, hard-packed ground.

"He's gone," I said. "Let's run!"

I sprang from the tunnel. Reese was right behind me, and we ran and ran and ran, our flashlight beams bobbing in front of us, darting around corners and rocks, heading out of the cave as fast as we could.

And it was a good plan, too. In fact, we would've made it out all right . . . but we hadn't planned on running into yet another mammoth . . . .

17

Up ahead, I could see light. Not bright light, but a hazy, gray light. I knew we were getting close to the mouth of the cave, and I couldn't wait. I wanted to get back to our campsite and tell Mom and Dad. Whatever that creature was, someone should know about it. I knew it was dangerous, and someone in the park could get badly hurt—or worse.

I sprinted another twenty feet and went around a corner, thrilled to see daylight streaming through the mouth of the cave. We were almost there!

But not quite . . . and when I saw what was standing at the mouth of the cave, I realized we weren't going to make it back to our campsite. We weren't even going to make it out of the cave!

Once again, blocking our way, was a mammoth. This was a different one, however, as its hair was a little darker. And I couldn't be sure, but he looked a little bigger than the one that had been chasing us.

I stopped running, and Reese ran into me.

"Hey!" he said. "What's the big—"

"Keep your voice down!" I hissed. *"It's one of them, but I don't think he sees us yet!"*

Reese peered over my shoulder.

"Now what?" he whispered.

"Back up, really slow," I said. *"We'll have to try and hide again. Maybe this one won't come into the cave."*

Once again, we found ourselves trying to hide from a mammoth-creature. This time, however, I thought our chances were better because the animal hadn't yet spotted us.

Slowly, we stepped backward as quietly as we could. Ahead of us, at the mouth of the cave, the strange creature was still looking the other way.

"Over here," Reese whispered as he tiptoed to the wall of the cave and slipped around the corner. He

vanished in the shadows. I followed.

I turned off my flashlight, and Reese did the same. The light coming in from the cavern entrance provided a murky glow, but, in the shadows where we were, it was quite dark. I wondered if the creature would see us if he passed by.

"I want to know what those things are," Reese said. "And where they came from."

"We'll probably get answers when we get out of here," I said. "Someone *must* know about these things."

Reese shook his head. "If someone knew about those things, they would shut down the park. Those things are a lot more dangerous than cougars or grizzly bears. Did you get any pictures?"

I shook my head. "No," I replied. "I didn't have time. Besides, I was shaking so badly that I don't think I could have held the camera still."

"Now what?" he asked.

"Let's just be patient," I said.

"That's what Mom always says," Reese said.

He was right. Mom was always saying things like 'good things come to those who wait,' and 'patience is a virtue.' Well, sometimes waiting is *hard*.

Like right now. I didn't want to wait. I wanted

out of that cave, away from that weirdo-animal, *now.* I wanted to be back at camp, with Mom and Dad, where it was safe.

However, if we needed to wait to save our lives, then I guess we could do that. When I thought about it in those terms, I really didn't have a choice.

As it turned out, we wouldn't be waiting much longer. There was a noise behind us, and we quickly realized the first mammoth—the one who'd chased us into the cave in the first place—was coming back.

There was a creature in front of us, at the mouth of the cave—and one coming up behind us.

We were in mammoth-sized trouble, to say the least.

When we first heard the noise, I couldn't tell where it was coming from. The earth trembled, but Reese and I thought it was the creature that was at the entrance of the cave.

We quickly learned different.

"Hey," I whispered, *"that sounds like it's coming from—"*

I stopped speaking when I saw a movement, and it was then I realized the mammoth—the one that had chased us into the cave—was coming back.

"He's going to see us!" Reese hissed. *"We're right out in the open, and he's going to see us!"*

But we had nowhere to run. We couldn't run out of the cave because of the mammoth at the entrance. And we couldn't run deeper into the cave, because a mammoth was coming out!

I was holding my flashlight in my right hand, gripping it so hard that my hand hurt. I switched, and held the flashlight in my left hand.

"The only thing we can do," I whispered, *"is stay as still as possible. We're in the shadows, and maybe he won't see us."*

"Sure," Reese hissed. *"That might be easy for you. But I'm shaking like a leaf!"*

Reese wasn't alone. I was trembling, too. I was scared. We were no match for creatures of such size, and I was sure we couldn't outrun them.

In three words: *we were trapped.*

The huge mammoth that had chased us came into view, lumbering through the cave. It was so big his head almost touched the ceiling. He plodded slowly, his trunk hanging down, enormous tusks jutting forward. His long hair was thick and matted.

So far, so good, I thought, as the creature passed directly in front of us. He was so close I could have taken a single step forward, reached out, and touched him.

And we got a better look at his giant feet, too. They sure were strange. His claws were long, thin, and slightly curved. Not including the size of his feet, each claw alone was at least four feet long!

Again, I wondered what on earth we were seeing. Was it some prehistoric animal that lived in the park? If so, how come I'd never heard or seen anything about them? I couldn't imagine the park rangers allowing people to go hiking in an area where these mammoth-beasts were. Sooner or later, someone would get hurt.

Reese and I both breathed a sigh of relief when the creature passed by without seeing us. For the first time, we got a look at his tail, which didn't seem out of the ordinary. In fact, his tail looked just like an elephant's tail. It was long, but not long enough to touch the ground. And it had a tuft of fur at the end.

"That's as close as I ever want to be to one of those things," Reese said. His voice trembled as he spoke.

"Same here," I whispered back.

"Now what?" Reese asked.

"We don't have any choice but to wait," I replied. *"Maybe they'll go away, and we can leave. We're not far*

from the entrance of the cave, so we can watch them and see what they do."

Both mammoths were at the mouth of the cave. They didn't do anything except look around. Their movements were slow, sloth-like.

Please go away, I thought. *Please, please go away.*

But that's not what they did. At the same time, both creatures turned and started into the cave, right toward us.

This time, however, I knew our chances of being seen were much greater, as the huge beasts were walking side by side, and each one was nearly touching the sides of the cave.

But they hadn't seen us yet. We were still hidden in the shadows, and I had a plan. Actually, it was the only thing we *could* do, unless we wanted the mammoths to find us.

We would have to sneak along the wall of the cave, ahead of the mammoths, before they saw us and chased us. True, we had no idea where the giant tunnel led, but maybe there were other places where we could hide. And, like I said: it was our only option. We could stay where we were, pressed against the wall of the cave, where the mammoths were sure to see us.

Or we could try to get ahead of them, unnoticed, and find a place to hide.

This will all be over soon, I thought. *Soon, we'll be back at camp, safe and sound.*

Yeah, right.

We weren't safe and sound by a long shot, and if I knew then what I know now, I would have never gone deeper into that cave. I would've taken my chances with the two ugly mammoth-creatures.

Instead, we went deeper into the cave. That, as it would turn out, was exactly the *wrong* thing to do.

Without explaining anything to Reese, I tapped him on the arm to get his attention. When he looked at me, I mouthed the words *come on*, and then I began slinking along the rock wall, deeper into the cave. I didn't even give him time to ask what I was doing, as I knew it would just waste valuable time.

After a few steps, I shot a glance over my shoulder to make sure he was following me. He was, and I kept moving along the rock wall, stepping around boulders and ducking around sharp edges that jutted out from the side of the cave.

Farther behind us, I could hear the mammoths

trudging along. However, they didn't seem to be in any hurry, which was a good thing. That meant they probably hadn't spotted us.

The deeper we traveled into the cave, the darker it became. I was still holding my flashlight in my left hand, and I clicked it on. A bright white beam illuminated the ground ahead of us.

"What are we doing?!?!" Reese hissed as he walked along side of me.

"The only thing we can *do,"* I replied. *"If we would have stayed back there, one of those things would have spotted us for sure. We wouldn't have had anyplace to go."*

"But we have no idea where this cave goes," Reese said quietly. *"What if we get lost?"*

"Getting lost is a lot better than getting squished by one of those things back there," I replied. *"And besides . . . this tunnel might come out somewhere else."*

We passed the small tunnel where we'd hidden before, but we kept going. I didn't want to be trapped in that little cubbyhole again, only to have the creature slime me with mammoth boogers.

Deeper and deeper we went. We moved cautiously, just in case we came across another mammoth. Two were bad enough, but I wondered if there were any more.

And we looked for other tunnels where we could hide from the two mammoths . . . and I couldn't believe our luck when we found one!

"There!" I said, pointing my flashlight beam into a dark hole in the wall of the cave. I shined it around, and it appeared to go deep into the ground. The mouth of the tunnel was big enough for us, but it would be too small for the mammoths!

We quickly scurried inside, only to find the tunnel didn't go very far, after all. However, it went far enough so that I knew the mammoths couldn't get to us, even with their long trunks and weird tentacles.

"We'll be safe here," I said, and I sank to the ground to rest. Reese sat next to me. For the first time in a while, we felt safe.

Not for long.

"They're coming," Reese whispered.

We could hear the two mammoths coming closer and closer. Not only were their feet making noise, but the animals were making odd grunting sounds. And, although I knew they couldn't get us in our small hiding place, I was still scared. I think you would be, too, if you were in a dark cave underground with gargantuan beasts roaming around.

But I started to plan what to do. I figured if everything went well, the two mammoths would pass us by. They would continue on, and that would leave the tunnel open for our escape.

And I started to think of anything that could go wrong. After all, if there were two mammoths, there probably were more. What were our chances of running into another mammoth on our way out? I had no idea, but I had to hope for the best.

The other thing that could go wrong is the two mammoths might hear us and come after us. I hoped that wouldn't be the case. I hoped that if the mammoths passed in front of our hiding place, they wouldn't detect us, and they would keep going.

"I wonder if anyone else knows about these things?" Reese whispered. *"It seems like somebody would know something about them."*

"We'll know once we get out of here and tell one of the park rangers," I replied quietly. *"Turn your light off."*

Reese clicked off his flashlight, and I did the same. Once again, we were wrapped in total darkness. I could hear the echoes of the mammoths' claw-like feet as they stomped the ground, coming closer and closer. It was strange. In the darkness, the sounds of their feet were all around us, and it was impossible to tell from which direction they were coming.

And without a light, it would be impossible to

know for sure when they passed by our hiding spot. Of course, they might *not* pass by. They might know where we were hiding and try to get at us, but I was confident we were safe . . . at least for the time being.

The thundering footsteps grew louder and louder. And then we could hear them very clearly, at the mouth of our small tunnel. The giant animals were still making weird grunting noises as they moved along . . . but they kept moving! In the darkness, we heard them pass by without stopping, and my hopes soared. It worked! We had outsmarted the two mammoths!

Reese was excited, too. *"They're gone!"* he hissed. *"We did it! We tricked them!"*

"Yeah," I agreed, *"but let's wait a couple of minutes to make sure they don't hear us when we sneak out. I don't want them coming after us."*

After waiting for a couple of minutes, I figured it had been long enough. We could still hear the mammoths as they traveled deeper and deeper into the tunnel, and the ground beneath our feet still trembled. But I was certain they were a safe distance away.

I clicked my flashlight on, and a white circle of light appeared on the cavern wall. Reese turned his light on.

"Ready?" I asked.

"I was ready ten minutes ago," Reese replied. "Let's get out of here."

We scrambled to the opening of the small tunnel where we'd been hiding and stopped. I shined the light in both directions and was glad to see only rocks and the walls of the cave. The mammoths were gone.

"Perfect!" I whispered. *"Come on!"*

We started running, certain we were finally going to make it out of the cave, certain we'd be back at our campsite soon.

Once again, I was about to be proven wrong . . . and it all started when the ground began opening up in front of us!

21

We had no sooner started running when we heard a rumbling sound ahead of us. We stopped—and just in time, too! In the glow of our flashlight beams, the earth in front of us—rocks, dirt, and gravel—began bubbling up!

"What's going on?!?!" Reese shrieked as we trained our flashlights on the growing mound in front of us.

"I don't know," I said, taking a few quick steps backward. Reese followed.

While we watched, I kept our flashlight beams trained in front of us. The ground was rising up, forming a large mound. We could hear and feel rumbling, and we took a few more steps back.

"Something . . . something's in the ground!" Reese stammered.

Whatever was causing the disturbance stopped. I moved the flashlight beam over the mound, which was now nearly as tall as we were and extended to include the entire width of the cave.

"I don't know what it is," I said, "but something caused the ground to do that."

"I want out of here," Reese said. "Let's try to go around it."

That seemed like the best plan, since we didn't see any more movement or hear any rumbling.

Wow, I thought. *What a strange day this has turned out to be! All we wanted to do was go for a hike, but we discovered a large cave and weird creatures.*

Suddenly, the rumbling started again, and the mound in front of us trembled and shook. A few rocks spilled loose, rolled off, and clacked to the floor. Dirt fell.

Reese and I watched, horrified, sweeping our flashlight beams over the mound and all around it, trying to see what was causing the disturbance.

Whatever it was, it was big, because the mound was still growing, pushing up dirt and rocks. By now, it nearly filled the entire tunnel in front of us. Even if we wanted to leave, we would have to climb over it to get out.

Suddenly, we saw something else: a short, curved spear broke through the top of the mound.

Then another.

They poked up and out and wiggled around.

Wait a minute! I thought. My mind was racing, my heart was going crazy in my chest. *Those are tusks! It's one of THEM! A mammoth-creature! They can tunnel in the earth!*

A bad day was about to get even worse.

22

All of a sudden, the mammoth's entire head poked up. In the beam of the flashlight, we could see he was a little different from the other creatures. The one coming up from the ground had a trunk, but the end of it was wide and spoon-shaped, like the blade of a shovel. There were no tentacles on it like the other two mammoths, and it looked like the animal used it as a tool to dig through the earth.

They're like giant mole creatures, I thought as Reese and I watched in horror. *They look like a cross between a mole and a mammoth!* Of course, I'd never really seen a live mole before. Where we live, we don't have any. But I've seen pictures of them, and I know they live underground. Moles are smaller than a rat, though. There's no way a mole could grow to the size of the creature we were now staring at!

And just what are we staring at? I kept wondering. *What in the world are these things?*

Suddenly, I realized that if I didn't shut off the flashlight, the creature would see us for sure. I quickly clicked it off, and Reese shut off his. Darkness enveloped us. I didn't like being in the dark once again, but we didn't have any choice.

I bumped into Reese. *"Step back,"* I whispered. *"We'll follow the cave back to our hiding spot."* It wasn't what I wanted to do, but once again, we found ourselves with no other choice. Sure, it had been a mistake to enter the cave in the first place, but we had to find a place to get away from the mammoth-creature. I never dreamed there might be more . . . or that they could tunnel through the earth!

Quickly and quietly, we back-stepped. Gravel scrunched beneath our feet. I didn't want to risk turning on my flashlight, but it was so dark I finally had to. I clicked it on and we turned around, following the white beam ahead of us until we'd reached the small tunnel where we'd been hiding. Then, we slipped inside once again.

"This is getting real old," Reese said, and he dropped his backpack on the ground and sat against the far wall. I joined him.

"We'll get out, don't worry," I said.

"How do *you* know?" Reese asked. He was frustrated, and I was, too. Frustrated . . . and scared.

"Because we're smart," I said, but I didn't sound very sure of myself. While I like to *think* I'm pretty smart, I wasn't sure we'd be any match for the creatures we'd discovered.

I don't know how long we waited in our hiding place. Reese and I didn't speak; we just listened. We didn't hear a single thing. Once, I thought I heard a rumbling sound, but it was so faint it could have been my imagination.

Finally, I figured we might as well try and make it out. If we encountered any more of the strange mammoth-creatures, we'd just have to figure out what to do.

"Let's go," I said to Reese. "Grab your pack."

We both picked up our backpacks and stood.

"Do you think it's safe?" Reese asked.

"I can't say for sure," I said, "but we can't stay here all day. Mom and Dad will come looking for us."

"That would be a good thing," Reese said.

"Not if those hairy things find Mom and Dad before they find us," I replied. "Come on . . . let's go."

We left the small tunnel, walking slowly and quietly. A few pebbles crunched beneath our shoes, but the sound wasn't very loud. We headed in the direction that would take us to the mouth of the cave.

Soon, we came across the place where the huge mound had been. I say *had* been, because the mound was now gone! In its place was a huge, deep hole that went deep into the ground.

"It's like that thing tunneled through the mountain," I said as I shined my light all around the hole.

"Good," Reese said. "I hope he tunnels all the way to China."

But here was the problem: the hole was so big it took up the entire floor of the tunnel, from one side to the other. There was only a small ledge of ground to walk on either side. We would have to be very careful to stay pressed against the wall of the tunnel and watch where we walked, so we didn't fall into the hole.

"We're going to have to go slowly," I said, taking a step around the big hole. I unzipped my backpack and put away my flashlight. Then, I slung my pack over my shoulder. "Stay close to the rock wall and hold my hand. Keep your flashlight beam aimed at the ground in front of us."

Reese slipped his pack onto his back and did as I told him. He grasped my hand and pointed the beam of light ahead of us.

We can do this, I told myself. *We can do this. Just don't freak out, Beth.*

Slowly, we started out along the wall. I didn't want to look down, but I had to, so I would know where to place my foot. We were right at the edge of the giant hole created by the creature, and I knew that one wrong move would send us falling, tumbling to who knows where.

"We're almost there," Reese said from behind me. He was still gripping my hand tightly as we crept along the narrow ledge.

"Almost," I said. "Just be—"

And that's when disaster struck.

23

We were only a few feet from making it all the way around the hole when the ground gave way beneath my feet. There wasn't time to jump, to leap, to do anything.

I was falling!

I kept a firm grip on Reese's hand, and he did the same. Had it not been for that, I would have been in a free-fall, tumbling into the black abyss. But he was still standing on the ledge, holding my hand.

"Don't let go!" I shrieked.

"I'm trying not to!" Reese screamed back. "You're heavy!"

"Put your flashlight down and use both hands!" I bellowed. "Hurry!"

Reese set the light down on the ledge, which was right near my face. Then, with his free hand, he grabbed my wrist.

My backpack had slipped from my shoulder when the ground gave way, and it had tumbled into the hole. I didn't care. In fact, at the time, I didn't even know that I was missing it. I was so afraid of falling that I couldn't think of anything else.

I reached up with my free hand. Reese had been holding my wrist with two hands, but now he released one and grabbed my other hand.

"Pull hard!" I shouted. "Pull as hard as you can!"

"I'm trying!" Reese said. "But there's not a lot of room here! And like I said: you're heavy!"

Reese was trying as hard as he could to pull me up, but he wasn't having much success. I tried to help by digging the toes of my shoes into the wall in front of me, but the dirt and rocks just broke away and tumbled down. Then, I tried to swing one leg up onto the ledge. I missed the first time, but on my second attempt, I succeeded in getting the heel of my foot on the ledge. Now, with Reese pulling my arms, I could help by using my foot. As long as Reese didn't let go, I might be able to pull myself up.

In fact, I had to. The alternative wasn't very appealing.

"I think I can do it!" I said. "Just hang on!"

"Hurry!" Reese said. "I can't hold on much longer!"

With a final burst of strength, I pulled with my arms and tried to raise my body up with my foot on the ledge. I felt a ray of hope as I drew nearer, but it was only for a moment.

Suddenly, the rest of the ledge gave way, and Reese and I were falling, tumbling into black, empty space!

Looking back, I should have known all along that something like that would happen. After all, if the ground had given way beneath *my* feet, it stands to reason that it could just as easily give way beneath Reese.

Both of us were screaming. Dirt and rocks were falling with us. Reese's flashlight was spinning out of control, and the beam of light spun around like crazy. It was like watching flashing strobe lights on a dance floor.

Suddenly, we weren't falling anymore. The tunnel hadn't plunged straight down like I'd thought.

It began to curve at an angle. In the next instant, I was rolling about, flailing madly and sliding down an incline. It felt like I was rolling down a very steep hill, but there was no way I could stop myself. The only thing I could think of was to grab something to hold onto, something to stop me from tumbling. But there was nothing.

I could hear my brother not far away, screaming his head off. When the ground had given way, we had let go of each other. He was close by, but I couldn't see him. In fact, I couldn't see anything except the frantic spinning beam from the tumbling flashlight.

A rock hit my cheek and it stung like a hornet. Dirt was in my hair and fell into my shirt and shorts. My leg twisted, and it hurt.

And we kept tumbling, end over end, head over heels, elbows and knees flailing out of control.

Reese had finally stopped screaming, and I tried to yell to him. It was hard, because every time I opened my mouth, dirt tumbled in.

"Reese!" I shouted once. Then, I spit out the gritty dirt that had fallen into my mouth.

"Help!" Reese replied in a choked voice. Although he sounded only a few feet away, I couldn't see him at all.

"I can't see you!" I managed to shout. This time, however, I was able to snap my jaw shut before any dirt could fall into my mouth.

We were still tumbling head over heels, but we were slowing, as if the tunnel wasn't quite as steep anymore. Still, I was super-scared. What if I hit a wall or a rock or something? Then, it would be all over.

Of course, things weren't looking good at the moment, either.

Suddenly, I struck soft earth. I say 'soft,' but it was still pretty hard. I landed squarely on my chest, and the impact knocked the wind out of me. My face hit the dirt, and sand went up my nose. Thankfully, I closed my eyes just in time.

"Ow!" my brother wailed as he, too, hit solid ground. The flashlight stopped spinning, and its beam shot up, straight and still. Dust and debris drifted through the saber-like light.

"Are you okay?" I said, spitting gritty dirt from my mouth.

Not far away, Reese made a spitting sound. I couldn't see him. "Yeah," he said. "I think so."

I rolled to my side. The flashlight was near, and

I picked it up. Another thing that was close by was my backpack, half covered with dirt. I picked it up, unzipped it, and pulled out my flashlight. With the two beams sweeping around, I quickly found Reese. I handed him his flashlight.

"This just gets worse and worse," he said, shining his light around. "How are we going to get out of here?"

I didn't say anything, because I felt like crying. I knew if I said something, my voice would crack, and Reese would know I was crying . . . and that was something I couldn't do. I mean . . . I'm his older sister. I'm supposed to look after him. I needed to be strong, even if things weren't looking good for us.

I swallowed hard. "We'll find a way out," I said calmly, surprised I was able to say the words without my voice breaking. "I know we will."

"Well, we'd better do it fast," Reese said, getting to his feet.

I swept the beam of light around. We were in yet another tunnel, only this one had been created by that strange mammoth-creature. And the tunnel was big, too . . . big enough for Reese and me to stand up. In fact, the tunnel was so big, I couldn't even reach the top of it if I raised my hands up! The creature that created it sure was big.

They tunnel through the earth like moles, I thought. *That's why no one has seen them. They live in the ground. Reese and I might be the only two humans that know these creatures exist!*

I shined my light down the tunnel, and all I saw was inky blackness.

"That's where we're going," I said. "It's got to go somewhere."

"Sure it does," Reese said. "It goes wherever that thing went."

"Well, we can't climb out and get back to the cave where we were," I said. "Let's just go slowly."

Reese finished brushing himself off, and we started down the dark tunnel. Here, the ground wasn't hard, but soft. My sneakers sank into the spongy dirt.

It was hard to believe we were somewhere in the ground, walking in a tunnel. And it was even harder to believe bizarre, giant creatures were the ones creating the tunnels. I wondered how many of them there were, and where they came from. It really was possible we were the only two people who knew they existed.

The tunnel twisted and turned, and, in some places, it was so steep we had to climb. The creature must have moved through the ground like an earthworm, turning here and there, going up and down, tunneling through the mountain.

Soon, we heard a noise coming from up ahead, and we stopped walking. I pointed my flashlight in front of us.

Something moved.

Something big.

Oh, I knew what it was, of course. But had the creature spotted us? If so, what would it do?

We were about to find out.

25

I quickly clicked off my flashlight, and Reese did the same. We listened, and I hoped the sounds we were hearing didn't get any louder. That would mean that the creature was coming our way, and, if that was the case, we would have nowhere to go.

Tense seconds ticked past. My heart felt like it was in my throat, and I could feel it pounding in my neck.

Bum-bum-bum-bum-bum-bum . . . .

The sounds faded. Soon, we could hear nothing.

"He's going the other way," I whispered softly.

"Too bad we can't go the other way," Reese

whispered back.

"The good news is," I said, "if he's going the other way, he won't be able to see us. Come on."

I turned my flashlight on and began walking. Reese also turned his light on, and we walked side by side. Our steps were slow and cautious, wary of the beast we knew was somewhere up ahead, hoping he wouldn't turn around and discover us.

Soon, we saw movement. I could make out the creature's tail and his two hind legs, pushing dirt away. Again, I was amazed at the size of the thing. It was like watching a giant chipmunk digging a tunnel through the earth. Once in a while, some dirt was kicked into the air toward us. When that happened, we raised our arms and covered our faces.

"Let's not get too close," I whispered.

"You don't have to worry about me," Reese replied. "I'm not going anywhere near that thing."

We were about twenty feet away from the creature, but I felt safe . . . sort of. As long as he didn't turn around, he wouldn't see us.

I had forgotten about the camera in my pocket, and I dug it out and raised it up. I quickly took a picture, and the flash lit up the tunnel for a split-instant.

There, I thought. *Now I'll have proof that these things exist. I have a picture of his tail and hind legs.*

I stuffed the camera back into my pocket. Ahead of us, the strange creature continued churning through the earth, pushing dirt behind him with his strange, claw-like feet. We were careful to move slowly, so we wouldn't get too close to him.

"I hope he digs all the way out," Reese said. *"I hope he digs all the way to the surface, so we can get out of here."*

I hoped so, too.

Suddenly, the creature vanished. One moment, we were watching his tail swing back and forth and his legs kicking dirt behind him. Then, he was gone.

We stopped walking. I turned off my flashlight, and so did Reese. Up ahead of us, we could see light. It appeared the creature had tunneled his way into a large cavern of some sort. A small amount of light streamed down from somewhere, and the air in the cavern looked hazy.

But that was all we could see. We couldn't see the cavern floor, nothing.

"Let's go see where that thing went," I said.

"There's light up there!" Reese hissed. *"That means we're almost out of here!"*

We walked through the dirt to the mouth of the tunnel, where it opened to a large cavern, which was all rock. On the far side of the cave, there was a large crack where light was streaming in. That was good, because, like Reese said, it meant we were close to being outside.

But when we looked down, we realized we weren't even *close* to getting out. If we'd been freaked out by what we'd seen so far, it couldn't compare to the sight we saw on the cavern floor . . . .

26

From where we were at the mouth of the tunnel, the ground before us sloped down. The cavern floor appeared to be a mixture of loose rock and hard-packed dirt. I could see large tracks where the mammoth had emerged from the tunnel and strode down. To the right of us, there were a bunch of large boulders that were taller than we were, that lined the cavern floor, like they had been pushed there on purpose.

But none of that was all that shocking. What shocked us was the fact that there were more mammoth-creatures—four of them—milling about on the cavern floor not one hundred feet from where we were!

"Holy smokes!" Reese whispered. *"There's more of them!"*

"Look over there!" I said, pointing. *"There's a small one!"*

On the far side of the cavern, what appeared to be a baby mammoth-creature stood next to a larger one. Still, the baby was big—probably the size of a rhinoceros. He had a trunk with tentacles on the end.

"I'll bet that the ones with the flat-shaped trunks are the ones who dig through the earth," I whispered. *"The other mammoths' trunks don't look like they'd be good for digging."*

We watched the creatures as they moved slowly around the cavern. They didn't seem to be in a hurry to go anywhere. One of them made a grunt-like, growling sound, but we couldn't tell from which animal it came.

And suddenly, we saw movement on the other side of the cavern. Rocks and dirt began to tumble away, as if something was boring through the ground.

Of course, that's what it was: another mammoth-creature was drilling his way into the cavern.

"This is the most bizarre thing I've ever seen in my life," Reese whispered as we watched the mammoth emerge. When the creature was fully inside the cavern, he shook himself, the way a wet dog shakes. Dirt and debris fell from his reddish-brown coat of fur.

And he had something in his mouth. We couldn't see very well because the light wasn't good, but it looked like he had twisted branches in his mouth. While we watched, the creature walked over to the baby. Using its shovel-shaped trunk, he began feeding the branches to the little one.

I must admit that, although I was still really scared, it was kind of cool to watch the mother or father mammoth-creature feed its young. The baby was taking the branches in his mouth and chewing them up. Soon, he'd eaten all the branches that had been fed to him.

I'd seen things like this before on television, but there was something fascinating about these strange creatures that lived in the ground, beneath the surface of the earth.

In fact, Reese and I were so caught up in watching what was going on in front of us that we weren't paying attention to what was going on *behind* us . . . until we heard a noise.

By then, it was already too late.

126

27

If we had been paying attention, perhaps we would have heard the mammoth-creature sooner. But we'd been so caught up in watching what was going on in front of us we neglected to think one of the things could be coming up from behind us, in the tunnel.

And that's exactly what happened.

By the time we turned around, the creature was already in view. I could see his tusks and his trunk with several tentacles at the end; his piercing dark eyes; and his enormous, claw-like legs. He wasn't moving fast, but I was sure he'd spotted us.

Now we were *really* in trouble.

I didn't take another second to think about what to do next. I grabbed Reese by the hand, and we ran from the mouth of the cavern to the nearest boulder about ten feet away. I didn't know what we would do from there, but we had to try and get away. Of course, while we ran for cover behind the large rock, we were in full view . . . and that meant the other mammoth-creatures could spot us.

We reached the boulder. From where we were, we couldn't see any of the animals in the cavern, and they couldn't see us. But they might have. And I was sure the one in the tunnel saw us, and he would easily be able to see us when he emerged.

Reese was all freaked out. *"We're going to be eaten alive by those things!"* he hissed.

"Shhhh!" I hissed back. *"We had to move! The one in the tunnel was coming right at us! We couldn't stay there!"*

I leaned back against the boulder, trying to make myself as invisible as possible—which was pretty hard to do, considering I had my backpack on. It made me stick out a few more inches than I normally would have. Reese saw what I was doing, and he, too, tried to press himself against the rock.

It didn't work, because the moment the mammoth-creature emerged from the tunnel, he saw us. He stopped in his tracks and looked at us.

Glared at us.

Okay, Beth, I thought frantically. *Now what?*

I looked to the other side of the cavern, from where the light was coming. It appeared to be a big split in the rock, and I thought we must be on the side of the mountain or some rock formation.

Back at the mouth of the tunnel, the mammoth-creature took a step toward us. Suddenly, there was a loud bellowing from one of the other beasts down below. The creature that emerged from the tunnel stopped and looked away. He turned . . . and began walking away from us! I couldn't believe our luck. He seemed to forget all about us and was now focused on joining the rest of the herd.

I heaved a huge sigh of relief. Not only had the creature been distracted, but, apparently, none of the other beasts had spotted us when we ran from the tunnel to the rocks. Now, we were hidden from view.

"That was a close one," Reese whispered.

"We were lucky," I whispered back. *"That's all there was to it. Look over there."* I pointed to the crack

in the rock wall. *"You see where the crack comes down? I bet we can make it over there by hiding behind these rocks. It looks like we would be able to climb up to the bottom of the crack and slip outside."*

"Hey, I'm all for getting out of here," Reese replied quietly. *"I've had enough of these ugly things."*

I peered cautiously around the boulder to see what the creatures were up to. They were just milling about and didn't seem to be doing much of anything, except for the littlest one. He was romping around like a playful puppy. It looked like he was trying to get some of the larger creatures to play, but they weren't paying any attention to him.

I looked across the cavern at the crack in the wall.

Outside, I thought as I stared at the light streaming in. *If we can make it to the other side of the cavern without those things seeing us, we can slip outside. We can get away.*

I had visions of what I would do when we made it out. We would race back to camp, where we would explain everything to Mom and Dad. We'd find a park ranger and tell him all about it. They would probably have to close the park down until it was safe. In fact, the park might not ever be safe. I was sure these strange mammoth-creatures, whatever they were, were much more dangerous than grizzly bears or mountain lions.

And boy, was I ever right . . . as Reese and I were about to find out.

28

"*I have an idea,*" I whispered to Reese.

"*That's what I was afraid of,*" he whispered back. "*Seems like every time you have an idea, we get into trouble.*"

"*Well, just listen to me, and we'll get out of here. If we stay on this side of these big rocks, we should be able to make it to the other side of the cavern.*" I pointed to the large crack in the wall of the cave. "*If we can make it there, we should be able to slip outside.*"

"*But what if they see us?*" Reese whispered.

"*I don't think they will,*" I replied. "*Besides, even if they do, I think we can still make it out in time.*"

Reese peered around the boulder for a look at the creatures. I did the same. The creatures continued to mill about, and the baby was still trying to get one of the bigger ones to play with him.

"Now's the perfect time," I whispered. *"Let's go."*

Reese didn't protest. I walked to the far side of the boulder and peered around it. The other large rock was only a few feet away, and with two big steps I was behind it. Reese followed immediately, and we hustled to the other side of the rock. Again, I looked down at the mammoth-creatures. None of them were even looking in our direction.

Again, I took a couple of giant steps and hid behind the next rock, followed by my brother. We continued to do this until we reached a spot where there was a large gap between the two boulders. Still, we'd gone more than halfway across the cavern, and the mammoth-creatures hadn't spotted us.

As the saying goes: so far, so good.

Reese and I scrambled to the other side of the rock. The next boulder was more than ten feet away, and we'd be out in the open for a couple of seconds when we darted out into the span. It would be our trickiest attempt yet, but as I looked out at the creatures wandering about, I didn't see any looking in our direction. The baby mammoth-creature had found a rock the size of a basketball, and he was using it as a toy, tossing it up into the air and watching it fall to the ground. He was actually kind of cute, in a mammoth-creature sort of way. I felt a little sorry for him, because he didn't have any other friends his age to play with.

"Let's get behind that rock as fast as we can," I whispered to Reese. *"But be careful not to make any noise."*

Reese nodded and didn't say anything. I shot one more glance at the small herd, just to make sure none were looking . . . then I sprang. I counted my steps to myself as I ran.

One-two-three-four-five-six-seven—

I made it!

I turned and looked back at Reese. He was getting ready to make his sprint, carefully glancing at the creatures to make sure none were looking. Then, he leapt out into the open and raced to where I was. He was running so fast he hit me and nearly knocked me over.

But in the next instant, we realized our plan

135

hadn't gone as well as we thought.

We heard a loud snort, and the ground began to tremble, and I knew we'd been spotted. I quickly peered around the side of the boulder to see what the commotion was all about.

The baby mammoth-creature was charging right at us!

Now, we were *really* in a jam.

I didn't know where to run or what to do, and by the time I decided we should try to sprint the rest of the way across the cavern, it was too late. The baby mammoth-creature came around the boulder and stopped. His head was down, and he was glaring at us.

We backed against the rock, terrified. Even if we tried to run, the baby mammoth-creature would be faster. There was nothing we could do but remain pressed against the large boulder and hope he would go away.

But that wasn't going to happen.

The creature looked at us. However, he didn't seem menacing or mean. Actually, he looked a little curious, like he was trying to figure out just what we were. He'd probably never seen a human before.

He took a step toward us, extending his trunk out as far as it would go. Those weird tentacle-like things swarmed in the air, sniffing, reaching toward us. The baby mammoth-creature was clearly curious, and I began to think that maybe—just *maybe*—he wouldn't hurt us.

"Hey, buddy," I said quietly.

The creature cocked his head to the side, listening.

"How are you?" I asked.

In response, the baby mammoth-creature took another step toward me, stretching his trunk out even more. The odd tentacles at the end of his trunk were only inches from my face.

Slowly, I reached up and petted his trunk, just like I would pat a dog on his head. His trunk was leathery, with short, stiff, wiry hair.

"How are you?" I repeated, gently scratching his trunk with my fingernails. His trunk curled up a little, and it seemed like he was enjoying the attention.

"You're a good boy," I said to him.

"You're crazy," Reese said.

I continued to scratch and pat the baby mammoth-creature's trunk. "I think he likes me," I said. "He doesn't want to hurt us. He's just curious. Maybe he'll just go away."

I stopped petting his trunk, and he took another step toward me, urging me not to stop. I could now smell him, and *wow!* Did he ever *stink!* I held my breath so I wouldn't puke. He might be cute, but he really needed a bath. But I began petting his trunk again, and he really seemed like he enjoyed it.

"Great," Reese said. "My sister's new ten thousand pound pet. What if he follows us home?"

"He's like a dog," I said. "He just wants attention."

After a few moments, the baby mammoth-creature backed away. He began pawing at the ground. Then, he spun around in a circle and made a few prance-like steps.

"He's all fired up, now," Reese said. "Maybe he'll fetch a rock for you."

My brother was being sarcastic, and he didn't realize he had a good idea.

"You know," I said, glancing down at the ground. "I wonder if he will."

Being careful to remain hidden behind the big rock so that the other creatures wouldn't see me, I searched the ground until I found a rock about the size of a softball. It was heavy, and I wouldn't be able to throw it very far. I drew my arm back and let it fly, up over the baby mammoth-creature's head. It clunked to the ground.

Sure enough, the animal spun and chased after the rock. It was interesting to watch him pick it up, because he used the tentacles at the end of his trunk. They wrapped around the rock and held it fast. However, instead of bringing the rock back to me, he drew back his trunk and tossed it into the air! It arced high and fell to the ground a few feet in front of me.

"So, he wants to play catch," I said. "Cool."

I reached down, picked up the rock, and tossed it again. This time, however, the baby mammoth-creature watched it. He took a few steps and actually caught the rock with the tentacles of his trunk!

"Hey, we could use him on our softball team," Reese said. "He's pretty good." I laughed quietly. In my mind, I could see the baby mammoth-creature on the ball field, wearing a baseball cap and jersey, catching pop-flies in the outfield.

Once again, the baby mammoth-creature threw the rock back to me. This time, it landed a little closer to Reese. He picked it up and threw it, and the baby beast chased frantically after it.

"We have to be careful not to attract the attention of the other ones," I said. "Let's wait for him to toss it back to us. We'll give the rock one more good throw, and while he chases after it, we'll try and run the rest of the way across the cavern. Just stay behind the rocks, out of sight of the other creatures."

We watched as the baby mammoth-creature chased after the rock . . . but he didn't pick it up. Instead, he just kind of pushed it around on the ground. When he finally picked up a rock, it wasn't the one Reese had thrown . . . it was much, much bigger, almost as big as a beach ball. Still, the baby didn't have any trouble picking it up.

"Hey, I don't like the looks of this," Reese said, backing up. I backed up, too, keeping my eye on the animal with his trunk curled around the huge rock.

"He's not going to *throw* it, is he?" I asked. But just as I'd finished my sentence, the baby mammoth-creature drew back his trunk and let the rock fly.

Unfortunately, that was the exact same moment that I tripped . . . and landed flat on my back. The fall knocked the wind out of me, and I was dazed. In fact, I was so dazed all I could do was stare up at the gigantic rock that was about to come down right on me!

30

The rock seemed to be growing larger as it plummeted toward me. Down it came, faster and faster. I knew I had to move, but I couldn't. I could hardly breathe, since the wind had been knocked out of me so forcefully. Besides: I don't think I really had time to move. I simply had to face the fact that the rock was going to hit me, and then it would be all over. I was going to get squished.

Suddenly, I was being yanked to the side. It was a violent move, and my shoulder felt like it was being pulled out of its socket. I could see the rock still coming down, down, down—

BAM!

It thudded to the ground right next to me. I was still flat on my back, but I had been pulled out of the path of the falling rock.

Reese!

"Beth!" he nearly shouted. *"Are you all right?!?!"*

I supposed I was.

"I . . . I think so," I stammered. It was hard to speak because I was having a hard time breathing. The fall had really been a hard one, and I was lucky I hadn't hit my head on a rock. But that wouldn't have been as bad as the giant boulder landing on me!

"Man, I thought you were going to be squished like a bug!" Reese exclaimed.

Now *there* was a pleasant thought.

"You . . . you saved me," I said with a gasp. "You saved my life."

"Nah," Reese said. "I just didn't want to tell Mom and Dad that you got hit by a rock and bit the dust."

That's my brother. Oh, I know he cares a lot about me, and I care a lot about him. He didn't want me to get hurt, and I knew it. And I sure was glad he did what he did.

144

The baby mammoth-creature remained where he was. It was as if he was waiting for one of us to pick up the rock and throw it back to him. Fat chance of that! The rock he'd thrown probably weighed two hundred pounds! There was no way in the world that Reese or I would be able to even *budge* that thing!

"He sure plays rough," I said, finally finding the energy to get to my feet. I brushed the dirt from my pants and T-shirt. My breathing had finally returned to normal, but my head hurt. Not bad, but I'd really hit the ground hard.

Problem was, we were in a world of hurt in other ways. All the commotion had attracted the attention of the other mammoth-creatures. Now, we could hear them storming our way, grunting and growling, their massive claw-like legs thundering across the cavern.

And there was nowhere for us to go.

31

I knew we were in big trouble. There was no way we'd be able to outrun the beasts, since the only place we could head to was the long crack in the wall . . . but we'd never make it there in time.

Then, I had an idea.

"Get down!" I hissed, dropping to my knees.

"What?!?!" Reese replied.

"Play dead! If they think we're already dead, then they'll know we're not a threat to them. Maybe they'll leave us alone!"

"You're crazy!" Reese hissed.

All the while, the ground trembled and shook.

I could hear the grunting and growling of the mammoth-creatures, growing louder as they drew near.

"It's the only thing we can do!" I whispered loudly. Resting on my knees, I bent forward and curled down, placing my hands over my head, trying as much as I could to form a ball. When I turned my head a little, I saw that Reese was finally doing the same thing.

"This is crazy," he muttered.

"It's the only chance we've got," I replied. *"Hurry up! Curl up like me, and then don't say anything. Don't move a muscle!"*

As the ground trembled beneath me, I wondered if we were doing the right thing. True, we didn't have anywhere to run . . . but what if the mammoth-creatures decided we might be a tasty treat? I didn't want to be a munchy mammoth morsel!

I could hear the herd coming closer and closer, but I didn't dare look. I remained perfectly still, as it was important to appear dead to the creatures. If they saw me move one single inch, they would know I was faking.

The grunting and growling stopped, and the

herd slowed. I was so scared I was almost shaking, but I forced myself not to. It was too important to remain motionless.

Around me, I could hear the mammoth-creatures. In fact, they were so close I could *smell* them. Their odor was totally gross. I guess when you live in the earth, you don't have to take a shower or a bath. Yuck.

They drew nearer. They were so close I could hear them breathing. I heard a few grunts and noises. Mammoth-creature talk, I supposed.

Then, I heard a louder sniffing, and I knew one of the beasts was checking me out with his trunk. In fact, I felt it brush my back, and I nearly flinched. Somehow, I managed to remain frozen in position. I hoped Reese was doing the same.

The creature that was sniffing me came even closer, kicking up dust. It filled my nostrils and, once again, I nearly gagged. Instead, I held my breath so I wouldn't have to smell the animal or breathe in any dust or dirt.

Please go away, I thought. *Oh, please, please go away. Please think that I am dead and go away.*

I felt my backpack shift, and I figured it was

being prodded by one of the mammoth's tentacles. Then, I felt a tentacle touch my side. One touched my shoulder and my bare neck.

Then, I felt another one wrap around my side.

And another.

And it was too late before I realized what the beast was doing. The tentacles had spread all over my back, around my waist, and over my shoulders. Suddenly, they tightened all around me—and the creature pulled me off the ground!

32

I almost lost it.

Almost.

When that thing pulled me off the ground and into the air, I wanted to scream . . . but I didn't. I knew if I did, the creature would know *for sure* I wasn't dead.

Instead, I allowed my body to go limp. When he picked me up, I let my legs and arms hang, and I kept my eyes closed. I managed to breathe a little bit, but it was hard because the mammoth-creature was squeezing me tightly. In fact, he was squeezing me so hard I thought he might break my ribs!

Higher and higher I rose from the ground, and I opened my eyes just a tiny bit. Immediately, I wished I hadn't, but I was so horrified by what was happening that I just had to see.

The mammoth-creature was holding me in the air, looking at me curiously. That was all. He was looking at me like I was some strange animal. Which, of course, to him, I probably *was*. I was probably as strange-looking to him as he was to me. He pulled me closer, and I was only a few feet from one of his eyes.

And what a big eye it was! It was black and glossy, bigger than a softball. A memory popped into my head, from second grade. My teacher, Mr. Keller, brought in a large, black stone called 'obsidian.' It was so shiny it looked like black glass. Mr. Keller explained to us it was made from volcanic lava, when it met with water. The lava was cooled very quickly, creating rock with a smooth, glass-like texture. Obsidian was often used as a gemstone for jewelry.

And that's just what the mammoth-creature's eyes looked like: black obsidian, deep and dark, endless. Staring into his one eye was both fascinating and horrifying.

Please don't eat me, I begged in my mind. *Don't*

eat me.

On the ground, I caught a glimpse of Reese. He was still curled up in a ball, motionless. With his pack on his back, he looked oddly like a giant turtle. But the other mammoth-creatures nearby didn't seem to be paying any attention to him. He was as still as a stone, and I was sure he had no idea I had been picked up by one of the strange animals.

The beast continued to stare at me, and I continued to play dead. My arms and legs hung in the air, limp, while the creature's tentacles at the end of his trunk gripped tightly around my backpack, waist, and shoulders.

Then, he set me down!

I couldn't believe it! I was sure I was going to be a mammoth-creature meal. Instead, he set me on the ground, and I laid in the exact position he placed me: on my side, legs bent, one arm flopped over the other in front of me. His tentacles released their vicelike grip. He gave one last sniff, and his trunk pulled away.

It worked! I thought. *They think we're dead! They're going to leave us alone!*

Next to me, one of the other creatures was sniffing around Reese. A couple of his tentacles prodded the back of my brother's head and neck, and I thought he was going to pick him up, just like I had been, but he didn't. Apparently satisfied with what he'd smelled, the creature withdrew his trunk.

And that was precisely the moment that my brother sneezed.

33

At first, I didn't recognize the noise as a sneeze. But when I saw Reese flinch a little, I knew the noise had come from him.

The mammoth-creatures stared at him. The one that had picked me up took a couple of steps toward my brother, who was still curled in a ball on his knees. The huge animal extended his trunk, and his tentacle tapped Reese's backpack, just like he was knocking on a door! If I hadn't been so terrified, it would have been funny.

The mammoth-creature began poking and prodding at Reese, who remained perfectly still. The beast then sniffed around with his trunk. He tapped Reese on the head with several tentacles. I think the animal was trying to figure out if the strange form on the ground was alive or dead. Hopefully, Reese would be able to remain still enough, and the mammoth-creature would finally ignore him.

Another one of the creatures strode up. He had a huge, shovel-like trunk, and he used it to try to wedge it under Reese. However, he only succeeded in knocking my brother over.

But Reese did the right thing: he continued to play dead. His arms and legs flopped out. He looked like he wasn't alive.

Still, the mammoth-creature kept prodding him with his shovel-like trunk. Then, the one with the tentacles began to poke at him. I was sure they knew it was Reese who'd sneezed, and maybe they weren't fooled by his attempt to play dead.

Another mammoth-creature came up to me and began running his tentacles on my head. It was so gross! I couldn't stand the thought of having mammoth boogers on my arm, let alone in my hair! I was so grossed out.

But then, the animal stepped back and left me

alone.

Reese, however, wasn't so lucky. The animal with the giant, shovel-shaped trunk was trying to pick him up.

That was the last straw for Reese. I had been hoping he would be able to remain calm, to remain still.

Not anymore. He'd finally had enough, and he freaked out.

"AHHHHHHHH!" he shouted as he got to his feet. *"AHHHHHHHH!"*

My brother had blown our cover, and now the mammoth-creatures knew the truth: we were alive.

We were alive . . . but not for long.

34

If only Reese had been able to keep faking it for a few more moments! I was sure all of the creatures would think we were dead and become bored. They would have realized we weren't a threat, and they would have left us alone.

But, I guess I couldn't blame him. After all, he *is* one year younger than me, and he *does* get frightened easily. Even I was freaked out when that thing touched me with his tentacles and lifted me off the ground.

Reese was on his feet, screaming like a madman. He started running around in circles, like he wasn't sure which way to run. Obviously, there was no place for him to go, because we were surrounded by giant, hairy, mammoth creatures. He looked like he was about to start running in one direction, then he would realize he couldn't . . . so he would turn frantically and look in another direction.

All the while, he was screaming like his hair was on fire . . . and that's what saved him. You see, the mammoth-creatures were so surprised by his behavior that they became frightened themselves. They'd probably never before seen a human, especially one acting like Reese.

The creatures stepped back warily, and soon they were thundering off, heading back to the middle of the cavern. Even the baby creature that had been so playful only minutes before, was spooked. He took off running with his tail between his hind legs, just like a frightened puppy. Soon, they had left us behind in a cloud of chalky dust.

By now, Reese had stopped screaming. He was frozen in place, holding his arms out, completely perplexed by what had just happened. It was almost funny to think about: a kid who weighed less than a hundred pounds scared away nearly a half-dozen creatures that each had to weigh several tons!

But I also knew this was the break we needed. With the mammoth-creatures thundering away, we now had an opportunity to sprint the rest of the way across the cavern, where we could slip outside.

"Reese!" I shouted. *"Let's go! Hurry!"*

We started to run, staying behind the wall of large rocks, zipping around small boulders. For the time being, I didn't pay any attention to the retreating creatures. I figured that, very quickly, they would discover we weren't a threat. Then, they would come after us. By then, I wanted to be long gone.

Of course, being that the creatures could burrow into the ground, they could *still* come after us, no matter *where* we went. But, it would take them some time. By then, I wanted to be halfway back to our campsite.

I stumbled on a rock and nearly fell. I caught myself, and we kept running. It looked like we were going to make it to the large crack in the wall . . . almost.

One of the mammoth-creatures had spotted us running away and was already in pursuit. I guess I didn't pay any attention to the trembling ground, as I was too focused on our escape. Now, just as we'd reached the split in the rock wall that would lead us outside, the huge mammoth-creature lunged forward, knocking Reese to the ground with his long trunk.

"Beth!" he screamed.

I spun. Reese was at my feet, and the gigantic creature was right behind him, bearing down on us. I reached down with both hands and pulled. Reese leapt up, but I kept hold of his arm and flung him forward toward the crack in the wall, which was just big enough for him to slip through. He made it! Reese was outside!

I was next, and I wasn't going to waste any more time. I leapt forward, but was suddenly jerked back. My feet left the ground, and I was suddenly suspended in the air, dangling like a Christmas tree ornament!

The creature had grabbed my backpack with his tentacles!

35

I was dangling in the air, completely helpless. I thrashed my arms and legs, struggling to break free, but it was no use.

Reese appeared in the lighted crack, carrying a baseball-sized rock. *"Let my sister go, you stinky, giant warthog!"* he shouted. He flung the rock, and it hit the beast square on the forehead. The creature didn't even flinch. It was as if he didn't even feel it.

The beast curled his trunk around, and I was now face-to-face with him. His glossy-black eyes glared menacingly at me. He smelled so bad I thought I was going to puke.

But I had bigger problems than his smell, and when he opened his mouth, I knew what was coming next.

I was about to be a tiny morsel for an enormous, smelly beast. His teeth weren't sharp, but looked more like human teeth. I was sure, however, his jaw was so strong that he was probably capable of chewing up a car. He wouldn't have any trouble with a small girl and her backpack.

He opened his mouth wider and pulled me closer . . . and if I'd thought the smell of his fur was bad, it was *nothing* compared to his breath! Ugh! It was so bad it stung my eyes!

"Let her go!" I heard Reese shout, and out of the corner of my eye I saw another rock go by. This one missed the creature altogether.

I kicked my legs and flailed my arms and heard a tearing sound.

Suddenly, I was falling to the ground! My backpack straps weren't strong enough to hold me, and they'd torn!

I hit the ground with a hard thud. Although I'd landed on my feet, I was so high off the ground that the force of hitting the earth caused me to buckle. I fell to the ground in a heap, but leapt up immediately . . . just in time to see the mammoth-creature devour my backpack.

That could have been me!

I wasn't hanging around a second longer. I ran to the crack in the wall where Reese was waiting.

"Hurry, Beth!" he shrieked. *"He's coming after you!"*

I dove forward, through the crack and into daylight. I nearly fell, but Reese grabbed me by the arm and kept me from tumbling to the ground. When I looked back, I saw the creature's trunk emerging from the large crack in the rock wall, twisting and turning like a crazed serpent. Then, it pulled back and vanished.

I breathed a sigh of relief and looked around. Before us was an enormous hill, composed mostly of rock. It wasn't big enough to be called a mountain, but it was still pretty large. That's where we'd been. That's where the creatures were living: underground, in their own caves and tunnel systems. It seemed impossible, but it was true.

And I suddenly realized it was raining. Not only was it raining . . . it was *dumping*. I was already soaked, but with everything that had happened, I hadn't noticed the rain. Dad and the weather forecaster had been right, after all. Dark clouds boiled overhead, and a lightning bolt tore open the sky, immediately followed by a peal of thunder. A strong wind whistled at my ears. It charged at the trees, causing them to sway and bend. My hair was soaked, but the wind was so strong it blew it all around.

"Let's get back to camp!" I shouted above the wailing wind.

But we had not one, but two problems. First of all, we didn't know where we were. I knew we'd emerged a long way from where we'd first entered the tunnel in the side of the mountain. For all practical purposes, we were lost in one of the biggest National Parks in America.

And secondly, a movement up ahead caught my eye. It was hard to see through the rain, but whatever it was, it was big . . . and I knew that our trouble with the gargantuan mammoth-creatures wasn't over just yet.

36

The storm raged all around us. Tree branches snapped, broke loose, and were sent flying through the air.

And in the distance, something large and brown was emerging from the forest. It took me a moment to realize what it was . . . but when I did, I gasped and pointed.

"Reese!" I hissed. *"Look!"*

It was a grizzly bear! I couldn't believe it! I'd never seen one in the wild before. The good thing was, he hadn't spotted us and was walking in the opposite direction, slowly and casually. He didn't seem bothered by the storm at all.

When the bear was gone, I started looking around. We had no idea where we were, and sometimes the worst thing you can do when you're lost is to keep walking. Then, you usually wind up more lost than you were in the first place.

However, this wasn't going to be the case. Reese spotted a sign on a post in the distance. We ran to it. It was a trail marker made of wood and displayed a trail map. Looking at it, we could easily see where we were and which trail we needed to follow to get back to our camp. The trail near the sign was easy to see, and we started out.

It was raining even harder now, and chocolate-brown puddles had formed on the trail. Reese and I were soaked to the skin, but I didn't care. I was just glad to be alive.

"No one is going to believe us," Reese said as we hurried along the muddy trail.

"Yes, they will," I replied. "That thing might have eaten my backpack, but I have my digital camera in my pocket. I have pictures of the footprints and one of the mammoth-creatures. Plus, we can bring Mom and Dad back here so they can see for themselves."

"I'm not going back there!" Reese said. "No way, not in a million years. I never want to see one of those things again."

The wind picked up even more, and I grew worried. We were out in a bad storm, and it might not be safe walking along the trail where there was no shelter. But I didn't want to stand beneath a tree, in case lightning struck. For the time being, the best thing we could do was keep going and make it back to camp as soon as we could. I knew Mom and Dad were probably worried to pieces and were probably out looking for us at that very moment.

A long, loud rumble of thunder rolled across the region. It was so strong the ground began to shake. But when it continued to grow even stronger, I knew it wasn't thunder. The only thing that could make the ground shake like that was—

One of those . . . those . . . things!

Somewhere nearby was a mammoth-creature. We couldn't see him through the trees, but as the ground continued to tremble and shake, I knew he was getting closer with every passing second!

37

"It's one of those things!" Reese shrieked. "He's coming after us!"

While we ran down the trail trying to dodge puddles, our heads darted from side to side. Soon, however, the trembling beneath our feet became so strong we couldn't run. In fact, when we stopped moving, the ground was shaking so much it nearly knocked us off our feet!

"It's not one of those mammoths!" I shouted over the wind and the rain. "It's an earthquake!"

I'd never felt an earthquake before, and neither had Reese. It was a horrifying feeling, not being able to catch your balance on solid ground. The earth beneath us rocked and rolled, and I was nearly knocked from my feet.

Thankfully, it didn't last very long. In less than a minute, the motion and rocking of the earth had subsided, and we could only feel the wind and the cool rain as it continued to pour.

"Let's keep going," I said, and we set out once again along the path.

It didn't take long for us to get back to camp. As I'd suspected, Dad was out looking for us. He was carrying an umbrella, walking quickly toward us. We ran up to him, and he didn't look happy.

"Where have you two been?" he demanded. "Your mother and I have been looking for you since it began raining!"

"We were attacked by giant mammoth-creatures!" Reese explained. "They were gigantic! As big as a house!"

"Uh-huh," Dad said. He looked at me. "Beth, maybe *you'd* better tell me where you've been."

"Reese is telling the truth!" I said. I turned for just a moment and pointed behind us. "Back there! We found these giant tracks, and they led us to a cave!

One of the creatures came after us and chased us underground! We just now got out!"

Dad looked at me like I was out of my mind.

"No, really!" I protested.

"Explain later," Dad said. "Let's get out of this rain."

The three of us trotted to Mom and Dad's big tent and went inside. Mom was angry.

"Where have you been?!?!" she said.

Here we go again, I thought. Just then, I remembered my digital camera.

"I have pictures!" I said, and I pulled out my camera and turned it on. "Watch! I've got pictures of the footprints, and I have pictures of the—"

I stopped speaking when I saw the message displayed on the small digital screen. In white letters, it read:

Error

"Oh, no!" I cried. "It must have broken when I fell, or maybe the rain got to it!"

No matter what we said, we couldn't get Mom and Dad to believe us. Reese and I told them everything, but they just shook their heads.

Thankfully, they weren't too mad. We hadn't been late for lunch, but they said we should have come back to camp when it started to rain. And they were worried when we had the earthquake, and we still weren't home yet. But no matter what we said, they wouldn't believe us about the mammoth-creatures.

Later, after lunch, we sat around in Mom and Dad's big tent. We'd put some dry clothes on, and around three in the afternoon, the sun came back out.

"Hey," I said, "we can *prove* what happened to us! We can take you to where we saw the tracks!"

Reese shook his head. "I'm not going back there," he said.

"Don't worry," I said to him. "We'll only go to the place where we saw the first few footprints."

Reese looked a bit wary, but he agreed to go.

"All right," Dad said. "We'll do it."

And so, we hiked the trail back to where I'd spotted the butterfly, glad I would be able to prove our story.

We were, however, in for a few more surprises.

I walked off the trail and looked for the footprints . . . *but there were none!*

"I don't understand," I said as I pushed a few branches out of my way. I scanned the ground in front of me and all around. "They were right here! The rain must have washed them away!"

"But look!" Reese said, pointing at a few broken trees and branches. "Those trees are snapped off because the creature walked through here!"

"It looks to me like the wind did it," Dad said. "It appears that—"

Dad stopped talking. He stared into the forest.

"What is it?" Mom asked.

"I thought I heard something," Dad said.

We all listened. Sure enough, we could hear the sound of something moving through the brush. I got a little nervous. After all, it could be anything: one of those mammoth-creatures, a bear, or even a mountain lion.

As it turns out, however, it wasn't any of those things. It happened to be the park ranger we'd met earlier in the day. And when he saw us, did he ever look shocked.

"What are you doing out here?" he asked as he approached.

"Oh, our kids think they saw some strange creatures," Dad replied. "I think it was just their runaway imaginations."

"Yeah," the park ranger said with a chuckle. He shook his head and smiled. "Kids these days."

He didn't believe us, either!

"We'll show you!" I said. "Follow us! We'll take you to where they live!"

I wasn't sure if this was a good idea or not, but we had to find some way to convince Mom and Dad we were telling the truth. Reese didn't want to go, but

I think he felt safer, now that Mom and Dad were with us. Even the park ranger said he would come along, just to make sure we didn't get lost. After all, he explained, we weren't hiking on a designated trail.

It only took us a few minutes to make it to the place where we'd spotted the first mammoth-creature. The mountainous rock formation jutted up into the cloud-splattered sky. But here was the problem: the mouth of the cave was gone! Instead, there were huge rocks and boulders where it should have been!

It was then that I figured out what had happened. The earthquake must've jarred the large rocks loose from farther up the mountain. They tumbled down, and they blocked the cave. I tried to explain this to Mom and Dad and the park ranger, but they just shook their heads. Mom told me I should just write everything down in a book, that it would make an interesting story.

So, we gave up trying to convince them. No matter what we said, what had happened to us was just too unbelievable. If my camera hadn't broken, things might have been different. They might have believed us.

No such luck.

Later that evening, after dinner, Mom sent us to gather more firewood. While we picked up dead branches from the ground, we talked about what had happened to us that day.

"It's too bad your camera broke," Reese said. "If we had pictures, we would have had proof."

"And that stinky, smelly, ugly giant thing ate my backpack," I snarled.

"I've still got mine," Reese said. "You can use anything I have, if you want. Come on . . . let's get this wood back to camp."

We turned around to head back, only to see the park ranger coming toward us. He waved at us, indicating we should stop.

"I was hoping to get a chance to talk to you," he said. "I want to talk to you about those creatures you saw."

"You . . . you *believe* us?" I asked.

The ranger nodded. "Oh, yes," he said. "I know all about them."

He began to explain . . . and I couldn't believe my own ears!

39

In talking with the park ranger, he cleared up a lot of things. He said the creatures have existed in the park for years . . . probably long before humans existed. He said it was most likely that, at one time, they were normal woolly mammoths that were common thousands of years ago. But, for some reason, it was suspected they were forced to go underground. Over the years, they had mutated into ground-dwelling creatures. They rarely, if ever, came above ground. He also told us the mutant mammoths ate the roots of trees, so they never had to come to the earth's surface.

The earthquake had most likely disrupted them. A few of them became confused and wandered about.

"But, how come no one has ever heard about them?" I asked the park ranger.

"Oh, soon the world will know," the ranger told us. "First, we want to know as much about them as we can. Once everyone knows about the creatures, people will swarm the park to get pictures so they can see for themselves. It might be dangerous, and we want to prevent that from happening. So, for the time being, we're all keeping quiet. That's what I'm asking you to do, at least for a few weeks."

"We can't tell anyone?" Reese asked.

"You can probably tell a few friends, if you want," the park ranger said. "They probably won't believe you, anyway. And you can tell your parents everything, but I don't think they'll believe you. Not until we break the news about the creatures."

Later that night, tucked in our sleeping bags in our tent, Reese and I talked quietly about our day. We'd been really, really lucky. Sure, that thing ate my backpack and my digital camera broke, but we escaped with our lives. That put everything into perspective, and I didn't worry so much about losing my stuff or my broken camera. Those things are just that: *things*. Things can be replaced.

I lay awake for a long time, afraid to go to sleep. I wasn't really afraid of any weird mutant mammoths attacking, but I was scared that I would have nightmares about them. Finally, I fell asleep . . . and I didn't dream at all.

The rest of the week was great. It didn't rain again, and we went hiking, fishing, bicycling . . . everything. Reese caught some big trout, and he was really proud. I tried my luck at fishing, but I didn't catch a single thing.

And we didn't see any more of the bizarre mammoth-creatures we'd encountered. Oh, I looked for them, that was for sure. I was always on the lookout, ready to run if I needed to. I wanted to be sure I saw them before they saw me. But not a single one appeared.

On our last day in the park, we had a lot of

work to do. We had to take down our tent, make sure all the dishes and pots and pans were washed, and pack everything up. It was a big job, but I didn't mind. I was a little sad, though. We'd really had a lot of fun on our trip, except for the day we were attacked by the mutant mammoths.

Reese and I got all our things packed, but Dad and Mom were still having a tough time making it all fit back in the van. Dad was complaining that every time we take a vacation, we always go home with a lot more stuff than we left with. Which, of course, wasn't the case this trip. We weren't near any stores, so we hadn't bought anything. And we certainly didn't take anything from the forest or the campsite!

So, while Mom and Dad struggled to pack the van, Reese and I wandered down to Kintla Lake, where we saw a boy skipping rocks in the water. Which was strange, as we hadn't seen any other campers all week. The park ranger told us the earthquake had scared most people off, even though he was sure they had nothing to worry about.

He heard our footsteps on the gravel and turned.

"Hi," I said.

"Hello," the boy replied. He knelt down, found a flat stone, and threw it into the water. It skipped twelve times!

"You're pretty good at that!" Reese exclaimed.

"I should be," the boy said. "It's about all I do anymore."

He didn't sound like he was bragging, not in the least. Actually, he sounded frustrated.

"What do you mean?" I asked.

"Oh, nothing," the boy said. "It's just that I stay away from toys, because I'm still freaked out. But stones don't scare me, so I spend a lot of time skipping them."

We talked a little more. He said his name was Eric Carter, and that he was from Murfreesboro, Tennessee. He was camping with his family, and they'd just arrived. They would be camping for a week, just like we did.

"I've never heard of Murfreesboro," I said.

"Have you heard of Nashville?" he asked.

"Yeah," I said with a nod. "I've never been there, but I've heard of it."

"Murfreesboro isn't too far from Nashville," Eric said. "Actually, I was born in Nashville, and now we live in Murfreesboro."

"But what was that you were saying about toys?" Reese asked.

"Oh, it's just something I have to get over," Eric said. "Something that happened a couple of weeks ago."

I was puzzled. *What could have happened to make him not want to play with toys?* I wondered.

So, I asked him.

"What happened?" I said.

"Oh, it's a long story," Eric replied. He picked up another rock and threw it into the lake. "I suppose I could tell you, if you want to hear it. But I have to warn you: after you hear what happened to me, you'll probably never want to go near a toy ever again. And you probably won't want to go into a toy store."

That's silly, I thought. But, I wasn't going to make fun of him. Besides . . . I really wanted to know why he wouldn't play with toys.

"Our parents are trying to pack the van," Reese said. "If I know my mom and dad, that's going to take them a while. Tell us."

Eric looked at us, then he sat on a rock. I sat next to him, and Reese sat on the ground by the water.

"It all started at a new toy store in Murfreesboro," Eric began. He shook his head. "If I would have only known."

He told us what happened to him and his friends, and he was right: after I heard his story, I didn't think I'd ever set foot in another toy store for the rest of my life!

NEXT IN THE
AMERICAN CHILLERS
SERIES:

#21:

TERRIFYING TOYS OF TENNESSEE

CONTINUE ON TO READ SAMPLE CHAPTERS!

The building sat vacant for years.

It was old, and there was a 'For Sale' sign in the window that looked as if it had been placed there a long time ago. The windows were dirty and grease-stained. My friends and I never paid much attention to the building; we'd pass it on our way to school, but we had no reason to give it any more notice than a casual glance. It was on Southeast Broad Street, sandwiched between *Captain Whipple's Famous Ice Cream* store on the left and *Lost Soles*, a second-hand shoe store, on the right. Dad said the old building used to be a hardware store. But that was years ago, and I never remember it being anything more than an old building in its final stages of disrepair. I suppose every city has a building like it, and I figured that one of these days someone would tear it down and start fresh. Maybe they would construct a new building and open a clothing store, or perhaps a book store.

I was wrong on both counts. The building wasn't torn down, and what opened in its place wasn't a clothing store. It wasn't a book store or a hardware store. It wasn't a restaurant or a deli or a dollar store.

It was a *toy* store.

Now, I have to admit, I was surprised. I thought the building would probably end up being torn down. But I thought a toy store would be really cool, especially if it wasn't just a toy store for little kids. I've been in some toy stores that have really cool things like model rockets and airplanes, games . . . all kinds of different toys.

My name is Eric Carter, and I live in Murfreesboro, Tennessee. I was born in Nashville, but we moved when I was very little. I've always liked it here. I like the people; I like the weather. I like my school and my teachers. I like my family. Oh, sure, sometimes my little sister, Madeline, really bugs me, She's four, and sometimes, she's a pest. But as far as little sisters go, she's pretty cool.

What I *don't* like are toys. Not anymore. Not since what happened at the toy store. But to understand everything, I have to start at the very beginning . . . the day something very strange happened when I walked by the old, decaying building downtown.

The day began like any other. It was summer, and it was hot. That's one thing you can count on in Murfreesboro, Tennessee: if it's summer, the weather is going to be steamy. I don't mind at all. Summer is my favorite time of the year.

I got up and went into the kitchen for a bowl of cereal. Madeline was already awake and out of bed. Still in her pajamas, she was sprawled out on her belly in the living room, watching cartoons on television. When she's watching cartoons, it's nearly *impossible* to get her attention.

I think the house could fall down around her and she wouldn't notice. Unless, of course, she couldn't see the television.

While I was eating my bowl of cereal, Dad came into the room. He's a mechanic for a car dealership in Murfreesboro, and he was wearing his dark blue pants and blue shirt with his name embroidered on it. My dad's name is Richard, but everyone at the dealership calls him 'Wizard' because he can fix almost any car. I know it sounds like I'm bragging, but my dad really is *that* good when it comes to fixing cars. His friends are always bringing their cars over to our house when they're having trouble with them.

"Hey, Big E," he said, ruffling my hair with his hands. That's what Mom and Dad call me: Big E. They've called me that ever since I can remember. They don't call me that *all* the time, but a lot.

"Hey, Dad," I said.

"What's up today?" he asked.

"Me and Mark and Shayleen are going

fishing," I said. "It should be a good day for it."

Mark Bruder and Shayleen Mills are friends that live on our block. Shayleen and I will be going into fifth grade at Hobgood Elementary this year; Mark will be going into fourth. We fish in a small ravine not far from where we live. Actually, it's only a small pond, and very few people know about it. But there are lots of fish in it, and some big ones, too.

"Well, bring home a couple of big fish for dinner," Dad said. "I'll see you tonight."

"See ya," I said.

Dad turned to the living room and looked at Madeline on the floor. "See you tonight, little lady," he said. Madeline just stared at the television. She was so engrossed in cartoons that she didn't even hear him. Like I said: when she's watching television, it's almost impossible to get her attention.

After Dad left, I returned to my bedroom, got out of my pajamas, and put on shorts and a T-shirt. When I returned to the kitchen, Mom was there.

"Did you get some breakfast?" she asked.

"Yeah," I replied. "I had some cereal. Can I go fishing with Mark and Shayleen today?"

"I don't see why not," Mom said, "but there's something I'd like you to do for me, first."

I hope it's not the windows, I thought. Earlier in the week, Mom had mentioned she wanted me to clean all the house windows, inside and out. It's not a really hard job, but it takes a long time.

"Can you run down to the store and get me a few things?" Mom asked.

Cool, I thought. *That'll be easy.*

"Sure," I said.

Mom scribbled a short list on a yellow piece of paper and handed it to me, along with some money.

"And I want change back," Mom said. "Don't spend it on candy, like you did last time."

"I won't," I said. "I'll be right back." I was glad Mom asked me to run to the store, instead of asking me to clean the windows. That would have taken a couple of hours, while going to the store would only take fifteen minutes.

I left our house and walked across the lawn. The grass was shiny and wet with dew. The sun was burning bright, and the morning was already very warm. Sprinklers sprayed water onto glistening green lawns. Hidden birds called out from trees. It was going to be a great day.

I walked up the block and rounded the corner. Soon, I was downtown walking along busy Southeast Broad Street. Like most mornings, it was filled with cars and trucks as people drove to work.

And I don't know how or why the old building caught my eye. I'd passed it a million times before, and I hardly ever paid attention to it. It always looked the same.

Today, however, something had changed. I noticed it right away, but I couldn't put my finger on just what was different.

I stopped walking and gazed at the dilapidated building. Traffic hummed behind me on the street, and I heard the tired sigh of a truck's air brakes.

Something is different, I thought. *What is it?*

I stared for a moment, until I finally realized something: the sign in the window of the old building had changed. For as long as I could remember, there had been a dirty yellow *For Sale'* sign in the window. The sign itself was every bit as grimy as the building.

Now, the *For Sale* sign was gone. In its place was a brand new sign, all shiny and colorful. I was too far away to read it, so I walked over to the building and stopped. I gazed at the sign.

Opening Soon! it read, in big, red letters. *Maxwell's House of Terrific Toys! The finest, most wonderful toys in the entire world! Strange and magical toys and games! You name it, Maxwell's got it!*

Beneath the words were cartoons of various toys: a Jack-in-the-Box, a rag doll with red hair made of yarn, a model airplane, and a train.

"A toy store!" I said out loud. "That'll be

awesome!"

And I really *was* excited. Not only was it going to be a new toy store, but it would be close to my house! I could go to the store any time I wanted!

I re-read the sign in disbelief. My mind was whirling, and I was so focused on the sign that I didn't even see the huge reflection of a monster in the window . . . until the thing was already upon me.

By the time I saw the reflection in the window, the thing was already lunging for me. I spun around to dodge the attack, but it was too late. Mark Bruder had already wrapped his hands around my waist.

"Gotcha!" he exclaimed as he squeezed once, then let go.

I turned and looked at his reflection in the glass. Because the window was so old and dirty, it made his reflection appear to be something it wasn't. In fact, Mark's reflection was much larger than he actually was. It had really freaked me out.

"You got me, all right," I said, and I pointed to his reflection in the window. "Look at yourself in the glass. You look like an ogre."

"Hey, that's cool!" Mark said, raising his arms in the air. His reflection in the glass looked really crazy, like he was ten feet tall!

"Ready to go fishing?" he asked as he dropped his arms to his sides.

"In a little while," I said. "It should be a good day for it."

"I just saw Shayleen," Mark replied. "She's got to clean her room. I told her to come over to my house in an hour, and we can head to the pond from there. Can you make it?"

"I'll be there," I said. "I've got to run to the grocery store for my mom." Then, I pointed at the window. "Did you see the new sign?" I asked.

Mark nodded. "I saw it last night! A toy store will be sweet!"

"For sure," I said. "I hope it opens soon."

We said good-bye to each other, and I started walking. I thought about the new toy store.

When will it open? I wondered. *What kind of toys will be there?* The sign said there would be all kinds of toys from around the world. It would be exciting just to walk through and see them all.

And I'd been saving money all summer. I do odd jobs around the neighborhood: mowing lawns, raking, things like that. I even opened up a savings account at the bank. Every month they send me a letter in the mail called a 'statement.' The statement told me how much money I had in my bank account. So far, I'd earned almost forty dollars since school ended.

After getting the items Mom needed from the grocery store, I started walking home. Mom didn't really need a whole lot, and everything fit into a single, brown paper grocery bag that I carried with one arm.

As I passed by the old hardware store, I again looked at the sign and wondered when the toy store would open. Maybe it was written on the sign, and I missed it when I'd read it earlier.

So, I walked up to the window and read the

sign again, looking for anything that would indicate when the grand opening would be.

Nothing.

I took a step to the left and looked at my reflection in the old glass. In the window, my form was distorted and large, and I remembered how freaked I'd been when Mark had surprised me.

And it occurred to me then, that in all of the years of walking by the old building, I'd never looked in any of the windows, and I had no clue what was inside the crumbling building. I had no reason to.

Now, however, I was curious.

I took a step closer and gazed through the filmy, grease-stained glass.

The building was empty, except for one very strange thing: in the center of the old store stood a doll. She had dark brown, curly hair with two blue ribbons tied in it. Her dress was also blue, and she was wearing matching blue shoes.

But, what was so horrifying was the fact that the doll was *moving!* Her eyes were blinking and her mouth was moving up and down! I couldn't be positive, but it appeared she was staring right at me. I could hear her speak, too, and I leaned toward the window and listened.

What I heard her say was nothing less than terrifying.

"*Eric,*" the doll was repeating, over and over again. "*Eric . . . Eric . . . Eric . . . .*"

My eyes bulged, and my jaw dropped. My arms went limp, and the bag of groceries tumbled to the cement and tore open. Items scattered around my feet, but I didn't even notice them. I was too shocked, too horrified to take my eyes away from the bizarre doll in the middle of the empty store.

"*Eric . . . Eric . . . Eric . . . .*"

A nightmare was coming to life, right before my eyes!

ABOUT THE AUTHOR

Johnathan Rand is the author of more than 50 books, with well over 2 million copies in print. Series include **AMERICAN CHILLERS, MICHIGAN CHILLERS, FREDDIE FERNORTNER, FEARLESS FIRST GRADER**, and **THE ADVENTURE CLUB.** He's also co-authored a novel for teens (with Christopher Knight) entitled **PANDEMIA.** When not traveling, Rand lives in northern Michigan with his wife and two dogs. He is also the only author in the world to have a store that sells only his works: **CHILLERMANIA!** is located in Indian River, Michigan. Johnathan Rand is not always at the store, but he has been known to drop by frequently. Find out more at:

www.americanchillers.com

Johnathan Rand travels internationally for school visits and book signings! For booking information, call:

1 (231) 238-0338!

www.americanchillers.com

All AudioCraft books are proudly printed, bound, and manufactured in the United States of America, utilizing American resources, labor, and materials.

USA